Darius Bell and the Glitter Pool

Odo Hirsch

Kane Miller
A DIVISION OF EDC PUBLISHING

First American Edition 2010
Kane Miller, A Division of EDC Publishing

First published by Allen & Unwin Pty, Sydney, Australia
Copyright © Odo Hirsch 2009

Library of Congress Control Number: 2009942475

Manufactured by Regent Publishing Services, Hong Kong
Printed May 2010 in ShenZhen, Guangdong, China

1 2 3 4 5 6 7 8 9 10
ISBN: 978-1-935279-65-5

To Rosalind Price
with an author's thanks

Chapter 1

Darius Bell walked through the grass. It swished at his knees, and Darius smiled as he went through it, feeling like a pirate plowing through a wide green sea. Behind him the clock tower rose above the house, and its shadow fell across the grass in front of him.

The clock in the tower hadn't worked for years. It was stuck on twenty-three minutes to nine, and had been for as long as Darius could remember. No one knew whether it was twenty-three minutes to nine in the morning or twenty-three minutes to nine at night, or whether that made a difference. Apparently the clock had a booming chime, but that hadn't worked for years either. In his whole life, Darius had never heard it.

In the distance he could see Mr. Fisher, the gardener. Mrs. Fisher was near him, and the two smaller Fishers as well. They were all bent over. When the Fishers were all out like that, just after breakfast on a summer morning, it wasn't too hard to work out what they were up to.

Ripe strawberries hung from little plants, row after row. They gleamed like baubles, bright and red amongst the leaves, weighing down their stalks.

Mr. Fisher straightened up at Darius's arrival, a pair of snippers in his hand. "Here, Master Bell," he said, handing him a large, luscious strawberry. "Tell us what you think of this!"

Darius didn't need to think too hard. Or at all. He opened his mouth.

"Smell it first, Master Bell!" cried Mr. Fisher quickly. "Smell it first." The gardener turned his face up, closed his eyes and demonstrated with a sniff through his large nose, which was perfectly adapted in shape and size for the task. "The scent, Master Bell, that's the beginning. First the scent, *then* the taste."

Marguerite, the Fishers' daughter, who was only a year younger than Darius, caught his eye and grinned. Her nine-year-old brother, Maurice, slipped a strawberry into his mouth while no one was looking.

Mr. Fisher watched expectantly. Darius sniffed the berry, closing his eyes, as instructed.

"That's it, Master Bell. That's the way. Tell me what you smell."

"Sweet," said Darius, sniffing at the berry again. "Fruit… Light…"

"Now take a nibble," said Mr. Fisher. "Just a little … from the end. Peck off its nose. That's it."

The fruit was still warm from the morning sun. The taste was like the scent. Light, sweet, the taste of summer.

Darius opened his eyes. "Perfect."

Mr. Fisher smiled.

"Better than last year."

Mr. Fisher frowned. There was nothing that pleased the gardener so much as being told that his fruit was perfect, and nothing that dismayed him so much as being told that it wasn't. Being told both things at once was almost too much to compute. Darius glanced at Marguerite and winked.

"Last year's were perfect as well, dear," said Mrs. Fisher hurriedly. "Isn't that so, Darius?"

Darius nodded. "Of course they were."

The frown stayed on Mr. Fisher's face for a moment, then he gave up trying to work out how both things could be true, and smiled again.

"I'll help you harvest them," said Darius.

"No need for that, Master Bell," replied the gardener, although he was only saying it, as he said it every time Darius volunteered to help, and it would be only another moment until he pulled out a spare pair of snippers. And it wasn't clear, when he did, who felt who was doing whom a favor. The gardener took such pleasure from the harvesting of his fruit

3

and vegetables that he couldn't imagine how anyone could fail to get equal satisfaction from the snipping of a ripe strawberry, or the extraction of a snowy cauliflower, or the plucking of a plump tomato fresh from its vine.

He pulled out a spare pair of snippers.

Mr. Fisher solemnly showed Darius how to select the strawberries to pick – only those that were deep red all over, without a hint of green even right up under the leaves, and with the seeds studded into the surface like tiny yellow eyes, and yet with a firm, healthy flesh; and how to snip the strawberry – no more than half an inch above the berry, and no less than an eighth, so the leaves of the fruit sat like a tiny stalked cap on its head; and how to lay it in a basket – on its side, gently, nestled in with other strawberries, so as never to bruise the flesh. He had shown Darius the exact same things the year before, and the year before that, but that didn't stop him doing it all over again.

For the next hour or so, Darius snipped. And ate, of course, just like Maurice, and Marguerite, who were both expert snippers and secret stuffers of strawberries into their mouths. You only had to stop chewing as soon as Mr. Fisher looked to check that you were still snipping and make sure that he didn't see any strawberry juice around your mouth, and hide the little stalk and cap of leaves from the strawberry under a bush, and put enough berries in the baskets so that it seemed as if you were making some progress. Even Mrs. Fisher popped the odd strawberry in her mouth when her husband wasn't looking.

Yet somehow Darius did manage to fill a few baskets before Mr. Fisher called the harvest to an end. He added them to the stack that stood in a wheelbarrow under a tree beside the strawberry field.

Mr. Fisher needed to get the fruit into his truck and off to the market. Other harvesters picked their fruit one or even two days before it got to market. Not Fisher. He insisted on selling his fruit on the day he harvested it. It meant he arrived later at the market than his competitors, yet he never failed to sell everything he had, and easily could have sold two or three times more. Those who knew him knew it was worth waiting for Fisher to arrive. Whether it was a bright red strawberry or a gleaming purple plum, to buy a Fisher Fruit was to fish a fruit at the height of ripeness, a fruit that had been hanging on the stalk only an hour before. Or three hours at the most.

The pile of baskets in the wheelbarrow was high. Mr. Fisher took half a dozen and stacked them in Darius's arms.

"Marguerite will help carry the rest," he said, and he gave another half-dozen to his daughter.

Then he pulled out one more basket and added it to the pile that Darius was carrying.

"This one's for you, Darius. For your work this morning."

Darius looked at the extra basket guiltily. "No, Mr. Fisher, I really couldn't…"

"I insist. It was a pleasure having you work with us."

"Really," said Darius. "The pleasure was mine."

"Nonsense, Master Bell. You'll take this basket and I won't hear another word."

Darius glanced at Marguerite and Maurice. They grinned. "All right," he said eventually. "Thank you very much, Mr. Fisher."

The gardener nodded, gripped the handles of the wheelbarrow, and wheeled it towards his truck.

Darius headed for the house. Marguerite went with him.

The last basket that Mr. Fisher had added to the stack in Darius's arms was a present, but the others that he and Marguerite were carrying weren't any kind of gift. Mr. Fisher lived with his family in the gardener's lodge, and the understanding was that he could grow anything he wanted and sell it at the market as long as he gave some to Mrs. Simpson, the Bell family cook. This arrangement seemed to work very well for everyone concerned, although it did mean that the grounds around Bell House resembled orchards and fields more than the estate of a grand mansion, producing just about every kind of fruit and vegetable you could imagine, and that Mr. Fisher was more of a farmer than a gardener, and didn't have time to cut the grass as often as he might have in those few places where there was grass left growing. But Darius, for one, couldn't see anything wrong with any of that. He would rather have strawberries than grass any day.

Mrs. Simpson, the cook and housekeeper, wasn't paid anything either, but lived in the cook's quarters with her husband and her three grown-up sons. The three sons went out to work each day and the Simpsons could have managed perfectly well if they had had to pay for their own house, but Mrs. Simpson had been the Bell housekeeper for so long that she couldn't imagine doing anything else. Besides, the Simpsons liked the cook's quarters. They included the butler's quarters, and the underbutler's quarters, and the maids' quarters, and the quarters of all the other types of servants who had once served at the House, and altogether these quarters added up to more than a large family residence. And of course Mrs. Simpson had the whole Bell kitchen to herself, which was more of a kitchen than any cook could ask for. Sometimes, just for fun, she baked cakes in the huge ovens of the Bell kitchen and sent her husband off to sell them to the cafes in the town. He collected miniature ceramic jugs with the money.

There were various other people who lived in and around Bell House. Mr. Bullwright and his family, for instance, lived in the big rooms above the garage behind the House, which he had extended and converted into a sumptuous apartment. From this apartment Mr. Bullwright ran a building company which did work all over the city. In return, he repaired the things that required fixing around Bell House, like the plumbing and the heating and the roof tiling and just about anything else you could name. An old couple, Mr. and Mrs. Deaver, lived in what had once been the buttery, and kept a set of beehives from which they produced a rich, dark, syrupy type of honey. Their beehives were dotted around all over the place, which was a very good thing, according to Mr. Fisher, because they ensured the pollination of his crops. The Deavers also kept chickens in what had once been the dairy, from which they delivered a supply of eggs to Mrs. Simpson.

It had never occurred to Darius Bell that this was a peculiar arrangement. Since there were so many places in and around Bell House where people could live, and since no one else needed them, and since everyone seemed to produce or do something that someone else required, it seemed to make perfect sense. He had tried to think of a better system, but he couldn't, and besides, he couldn't work out what was wrong with this one in the first place. Yet he knew perfectly well that it was unlike the way things were done by most people, who paid for their needs with money rather than by offering places to live. Not that his parents never bought things with money. They did. Only not very often.

And that, of course, occasionally did create problems.

The fragrant scent of the strawberries wafted up from the baskets that he and Marguerite were carrying as they headed for the House.

"Come on," said Darius, suddenly. "Let's have mine."

"I don't think I could eat a single one more," said Marguerite.

"Of course you could."

"Anyway, they're yours. They're not for me."

As if all the strawberries he had eaten while he harvested

were for *him*, thought Darius. He sat down in the grass. "Here," he said, holding out the basket.

Marguerite shook her head.

"I won't eat one until you do."

"You will. You can't resist!"

Darius shook his head. Still he held the basket out.

Marguerite hesitated. Finally she sat down and took one. Darius took one as well. Then another. So did Marguerite, who seemed to have recovered her ability to eat them. The strawberries were big, firm, luscious. Soon the basket was empty.

"Definitely better than last year," said Darius.

"True, except last year's were perfect as well," said Marguerite.

They looked at each other, and then both burst out laughing.

"Your father's funny," said Darius.

Marguerite nodded.

"I wonder what he'd do if there was no fruit in the world."

Marguerite frowned at that. "I think he'd have to invent it."

How would you invent a strawberry? Darius gazed at the empty basket. He wished he could invent one right now. Or two, perhaps. He glanced at the other baskets, all full of berries. But if he and Marguerite started on those, there was no telling when they would stop.

Marguerite rested back on her elbows. She gazed at the clock tower above the House. "What's happening with the Gift?" she asked.

"It's almost ready," said Darius.

"What is it? Everyone's trying to guess."

"It's a surprise."

"But it's due in a month." Marguerite glanced at him. "You must know what it is."

Darius shook his head.

"I bet you do. You can tell me. I won't tell anyone else."

"It's a surprise, Marguerite."

"I bet you've told your friends. I bet you've told Oliver and Paul."

"I haven't." Not that they didn't want to know. His two best friends, Oliver Roberts and Paul Klasky, had been bugging him for months to find out. "Papa hasn't told me what it is. He hasn't told anyone."

Marguerite gazed at him skeptically.

Darius laughed. "It's true!"

"I don't believe you, Darius."

"Well, it's the truth. But it's going to be fantastic. It's going to be the best Gift ever."

"That's what everyone's saying."

"It will be."

Marguerite looked at him pleadingly. "Can't you tell me? I won't tell anyone. I promise."

"I don't know! Honestly, Marguerite, I'd like to know just as much as you would."

"You couldn't," said Marguerite.

Darius laughed again. "It's been twenty-five years since the last Gift. Surely we can wait one month more!"

Chapter 2

Mrs. Simpson had used the strawberries to make a pie. She brought it in after lunch, still warm, for dessert. They were eating in the blue dining room. The wallpaper in the blue dining room had once been a striking blue, like the sky on a sunny, perfectly cloudless day, and it was still blue, but rather faded, like the sky on that same sunny day at the very end of the afternoon. Yet of all the dining rooms in the House – and there were at least five, and possibly six if you included the tangerine room, which was large enough for only four people – the blue dining room was Darius's father's favorite. Consequently all the unbroken dining chairs were in there, and if you wanted to eat in any of the other rooms you had to carry your own chair with you.

Darius's father savored the pie. "Excellent," he pronounced, after taking a bite and considering it carefully. "Light, sweet, flavorsome. And the color of these strawberries. The color! Not to mention the flavor and the scent. Do you know what they remind me of ?" Darius's father paused dramatically, looking around the room with wide eyes, holding his fork in the air.

"What?" said Darius's mother.

"The strawberries I had when I was a boy when we went on holiday to the mountains of Greece."

"I didn't know they had strawberries in the mountains of Greece," said Mrs. Simpson, who had waited in the dining room to see what people thought of her pie.

"It may have been France," said Darius's father, with a wave of his fork. "They're perfect, Mrs. Simpson. My compliments to Mr. Fisher. But most importantly, my compliments to you. To grow strawberries such as these is one thing, but to cook them like this is another. You haven't merely captured their essence, but magnified it, intensified it, in short, *electrified* it. And yet…" he paused once again, waving his fork once for emphasis, "there's not a hint of the berries being overcooked. Of all the admirable things you have achieved in this pie, Mrs. Simpson, of all the notable features, of all the exquisite sensations, this is the one that will linger with me forever. Not a hint of overcooking! You, more than anyone, Mrs. Simpson, must know how easy it is to overcook a strawberry in a pie."

Mrs. Simpson nodded. "I do, Mr. Bell."

"Exactly! Remember that, Cyrus," said Darius's father seriously, speaking to Darius's older brother.

Cyrus rolled his eyes. He refused to answer to the name Cyrus, which he hated, and demanded to be called Robert instead. Robert, he insisted, was a normal name, and Cyrus was ridiculous. Yet he couldn't quite keep to his own rules. "Why should I remember that?" he muttered. "I'm never going to be a cook."

Darius's father laughed. "You never know! You never know, Cyrus. Isn't that true, Micheline?"

Darius's mother nodded. "You never know."

"What?" demanded Cyrus.

"That's the point!" exclaimed Darius's father. "You never know that, either!"

Cyrus shook his head impatiently. He glanced at Darius, who shrugged. Darius ate the pie. It was excellent, just as his father said. Darius wasn't sure about the rest of it. His father, whose name was Hector, had a tendency to talk enthusiastically – some said even exaggeratedly – about almost anything, and was quite capable of turning something that most people would have said in a single sentence into a twenty-minute speech. Or as Darius had once heard his mother remark in a moment of exasperation, Hector Bell never used one word when three would do. And as for the things his father had seen and done and tasted as a boy in the mountains of Greece, or France, or Austria, or Canada, or

Guatemala, or any other country that came to mind, Darius had heard so many stories that he had begun to suspect his father had actually been to very few of those mountains, or if he had, that he had no idea anymore which were which. And yet there always seemed to be a grain of truth in what his father said, even if it sometimes took an awfully long time to find it. Because it probably *was* very easy to overcook a strawberry, thought Darius, as he ate another piece, and Mrs. Simpson certainly hadn't done that. And he ate yet another piece, just to be sure.

"Well, there are some things I *do* know," said Cyrus. "Everything's arranged. I got the letter from the university yesterday."

His parents glanced at each other.

"That's nice, dear," said Darius's mother.

Darius's father didn't say anything, but only frowned slightly. Cyrus was six years older than Darius and he was planning to go to university after the summer holiday. He had decided he was going to study to be an engineer and then he would get a job building things, as engineers do. Darius's father hadn't exactly opposed the plan, although he hadn't exactly supported it either. It wasn't the idea of Cyrus going to university that worried him. Hector Bell expected his sons to go to university. After all, he had gone to university himself, where he had studied English Literature and where he had met Darius's mother, who studied English Literature as well. It wasn't even the idea of Cyrus studying Engineering that worried him. It was the idea of him getting a job afterwards.

The Bells – or the Arbuthnot-Huntingdon-Castleton-Bells, to give them their full name – as a rule didn't get jobs. They didn't work in business, or practice law, or carry out any other activities of a commercial or industrial nature. Traditionally, they had been statesmen and generals. Darius's great-great-great-great-great-great-grandfather had fought at Waterloo, and another ancestor had fought in the Mexican Revolution, first on one side and then on another. One of his great-great-great-great-great-uncles had signed the Treaty of Anchorage, and another had been a witness to the surrender of Queenstown, and had been its Governor for twenty years. Consequently, the Bells had been showered with honors, rewards and grants of land from one government after another, and at one point had been one of the wealthiest families in the country. Yet there was only so much wealth to go around, and families have a habit of getting bigger. And there hadn't been a famous statesman or general in the family for years. And if the rewards stop coming, and if you do very little of a commercial or industrial nature – or very little of anything, in fact, except write short stories for your own amusement, which seemed to be all that Darius's father did – and if you have to start living from the savings you inherited, then at some point money will start to be in short supply.

This was a point that had been reached by Darius's father some years earlier, even before Darius had been born. It was then that he discovered that Mr. Fisher would farm the land around the House in return for a small proportion of his produce, and Mrs. Simpson would happily stay on if her whole family, including a few stray relatives who appeared from time to time, could live at the House, and Mr. Bullwright would continue doing odd repairs if he could fix up the apartment above the garage for his own use and run a building business from it, and old Mr. and Mrs. Deaver were quite happy to live in the buttery if they could scatter their beehives around the grounds. Since there were very few left of the army of servants who had once worked in the House, it seemed a perfectly sensible arrangement. In fact, it was more than sensible, and appealed to Hector Bell's literary nature. The House and its grounds would be like a small town in its own right, a town within a town, and no doubt would furnish him with a wealth of ideas and anecdotes for his short stories. With the small amount he had left over from the money he had inherited, and the contributions of all the people who lived around the House, the family could just get by. Most importantly, they could continue living in the House with a cook and a gardener and various other people here and there, just as the family had lived during the grand days of the Bells. Or almost as they had lived, plus or minus a few servants, and a lick of paint, and new clothes, and a car that didn't break down all the time. In short, they could still uphold the honor of the Bell family name, at least to external appearances.

"Well, Cyrus, you haven't even started your degree," said Darius's father eventually. "It's a long time yet until you finish.

Who knows what you'll decide to do?"

"You won't stop me, Papa! I will get a job. I want to build things."

"You can build things here," said Darius's mother. "Like your models."

"My models are only for practice."

"You can build as a hobby," said his father.

"No! I'm not going to build as a hobby. I'm going to get a job and I'm going to build things that people will really use and I'm going to be paid as well. For once I'm going to have some money. At least one of us in this family will!"

Darius's father frowned slightly, as if he had just felt a pain somewhere. There was silence. Then Hector Bell turned to Darius.

"Remember, Darius," he said, "it doesn't matter how much money you've got, you've always got the family name. That's much more important. You'll always be a Bell, and you must never forget it. No one can take that away from you."

"Who cares?" demanded Cyrus.

"Cyrus!" said his mother.

"I don't care about the name! Arbuthnot-Huntingdon-Castleton-Bell! What does it mean, anyway? I don't care about the name if it means I have to live in this big mausoleum with peeling paint and broken stairs. I'm going to build things that are new and strong. I'm going to get a job and be paid for it just like any other person."

"Cyrus!" said his mother again.

"What? It's the truth. And we won't even get to stay in this mausoleum if you can't produce a Gift. They'll throw us out. There's only a month to go. Where is it? What's it going to be?"

"It's a surprise, Cyrus. Your father told you."

"Is it?" demanded Cyrus. "Where's the Gift going to come from, Papa? Where? Where's the money for it?"

"It's going to be a surprise, Cyrus," said Hector Bell. "Just you wait, when you finally see it…"

But Cyrus didn't wait. He jumped up and stormed out of the blue dining room, slamming the door behind him.

Darius's father stared at the door. Then he glanced at Darius. He gave him a smile.

Darius smiled back. But he wasn't sure what he was smiling about. For weeks his father had been telling him the Gift was going to be a surprise. What was going on? Was there a problem?

Chapter 3

Darius didn't know what a mausoleum was, but from the way Cyrus had said it, he suspected it wasn't very pleasant. And if that was the case, he disagreed with his brother. He loved the House.

He knew it wasn't in a very good state. The houses of his friends were in much better condition. The clock in the clock tower didn't work, and never had for as far back as Darius could remember. But which of his friends even had a clock tower? As for the rest of the House, the paint was peeling, and the stairs creaked and the banisters were loose and there were places where the floorboards sagged alarmingly under your feet. In some of the deserted rooms they were broken through entirely. And yet Darius didn't mind. If anything, it just made him like the House even more. Besides, even if Darius had cared about the state of the place, there were so many wonderful and unexpected things about it that a bit of peeling paint and a few creaking floorboards, and the odd spot in the roof where the tiles had come loose, and a number of cracks in the windows that no one had gotten around to fixing, and the various other things that went wrong from time to time and never seemed to get repaired, wouldn't have counted for anything. Because there were all kinds of rooms in the House, and all kinds of things in the rooms, and you wouldn't find those at any of his friends' houses, no matter how modern and well-kept they were. And the proof of it was that Darius's friends always wanted to come to his place and they hardly ever went to anyone else's house.

For a start, there was the clock tower, of course. That was one of Darius's favorite spots. But he rarely took his friends up there. It was a place where he went by himself. He would climb the tower when he wanted to think, right up to the roof above the clock, from which he could see the whole of the estate and the streets beyond. Or there was the echo gallery. Now, that was a place to take people! It was almost a hundred feet long, and the floor was of a special grey stone and the walls and the ceiling of a special hardened wood, which made sound bounce off them without losing any of its amplitude. At least, that was Cyrus's explanation, and Cyrus was rarely mistaken when it came to scientific matters. You could stand at one end of the echo gallery and whisper and someone at the other end could hear you as if you were talking into his ear. But put Darius and half a dozen of his friends in there, and there wasn't much whispering! It was also long enough to have a football game, which was an added attraction. They were the noisiest games ever.

The whole west wing of the House was empty, with pictures of long-dead Bells in old-fashioned clothes and old-fashioned cars, or even carriages, and you could play terrifying games of hide-and-seek that went on for hours, with people rearing up at you from under the dusty dustcovers of ancient, broken furniture and scaring the life out of you. Or you out of them. Or you could go outside and ramble over the grounds of the estate beyond the areas where Mr. Fisher grew his fruits and vegetables. There was a lake, where Mr. Gardiner, one of the fishmongers in the town, cultivated fish in return for a proportion of his catch. Consequently, the pond was teeming with carp, trout, pike, crayfish and all kinds of freshwater creatures. Beyond the lake was a small wood. Mr. Ostrovich, one of the carpenters in the town, was allowed to come and chop down three of the great oaks in the wood of the Bell Estate each year – the timber from which made the most wonderful tables and chairs – in return for repairing furniture in the House. Not all the furniture, of course – repairing everything that needed fixing would have taken all of Mr. Ostrovich's time, and fresh breaks were always happening as soon as older ones were fixed – but at least the most important pieces.

In the middle of the wood was a garden house built out of stone. It was like a large, single room that was open on one side, and in front of it stood a stone fountain in the shape of a boy and a girl dancing, with frogs and fish around their feet. When it had been working, the water must have risen in little jets out of the mouths of the animals, and the boy and girl must have seemed to be dancing on water. But the fountain had stopped working at some time long in the past. Originally the fountain had stood in a clearing, but this was now overgrown with nettles and wild rose, almost hiding the fountain from view. The garden house itself was half-buried in bushes and vines, like an ancient temple in a tropical jungle, and it would have been almost impossible to get to it but for a tree that had crashed to the ground and still lay there, a gigantic, rotting log, providing a kind of walkway through the undergrowth. Lizards ran in and out of the house, and birds flew suddenly out of the trees when anyone approached. Darius and his friends liked to go there, just as Cyrus and his friends had when they were Darius's age, and as generations of Bell children had done before. They would get food from Mrs. Simpson – cake or scones or anything else she had, and sometimes a whole picnic – and they would walk along the slippery, mossy surface of the log, daring each other to go faster, or to cross the log with their eyes closed, and then they would sit in the jungle house, as they called it, sharing their food and making up stories about what the house might have been used for, and what might have happened in it, some of which were so scary they almost curdled the blood.

Yet all of this, the echo gallery and the west wing and the clock tower and the jungle house and the hundred and one other nooks and crannies that Darius knew and loved in Bell House all depended on one thing: the Bell Gift.

The tradition of the Gift went back over a hundred years, to the time when the city council had given the land for Bell House to Darius's great-great-great-great-great-grandfather, Cornelius Bell, in recognition of the statesman-like work he had done at the time the city was founded. But any great statesman makes enemies, or at least people who are jealous of him, and this was no less true of Cornelius Bell than of anyone else. Some members of the council objected to the idea of giving him so great a reward, and in reality wanted to give him nothing. Instead of a large tract of land, they suggested that Cornelius Bell be given a small silver vase, so small, in fact, that it would be more of an insult than a tribute. Those in the middle of the dispute wanted to make the grant of the land, but only in return for payment. And the supporters of Cornelius Bell thought that even the land under discussion was too small a reward, and an even greater grant was required. No party had enough votes on the council to get its way and the dispute dragged on amidst great debates, almost coming to blows on more than one occasion. At last, when it seemed there was no way out of the dilemma, an elderly lawyer called Everard Hoover made a proposal: Cornelius Bell would be given the land, and yet he would be asked to pay, and yet the payment would be made but once in a generation, every twenty-five years, and the sum and the type of the payment would be entirely up to Cornelius Bell himself and the Bell descendant who would be responsible whenever the payment came due. This proposal united the supporters of Cornelius Bell and those in the middle, and even one or two of his enemies, now utterly sick of the struggle, and so the vote was carried. A month later, the land was given to Cornelius Bell, and in return, Cornelius Bell made the first of the Bell Gifts, as the once-in-a-generation payment came to be known.

The Gift that Cornelius Bell gave was an enormous marble statue of himself on horseback that he had had made by the finest sculptor in Italy and put up in Founders Square, in the very center of the town. No one doubted that the square needed decoration, but not all were sure that a statue of oneself was the most tasteful gift to give. It certainly wasn't modest. The second Bell Gift, made twenty-five years later by Cornelius's son, was a soaring copper spire for the tower of the town hall overlooking Founders Square, topped by a weather vane in the shape of a man ringing a bell, so as to remind everyone where the gift came from. The third Bell Gift was a stupendous bronze bell to go in the tower, which became known as the Bell Bell, and which produced an additional reminder of the Bells every hour, just in case the statue and the spire weren't enough. The fourth Bell Gift was a fountain that was installed in Founders Square diagonally opposite the statue of Cornelius Bell, with a basin in the shape of an upturned bell. And the fifth Bell Gift was a set of magnificent stained glass windows made for the council chamber in the town hall under the Bell Spire and the Bell Bell. Just in case anyone missed all the Bell hints around the square, the windows showed the greatest exploits of the members of the Bell family, starting with the Bell who had fought at Waterloo. But by the time this Gift was given, these exploits were far in the past, and the Bell fortune was dwindling. There were twelve windows in the council chamber, but only eight were filled with stained glass, and the two at either end were left as they were. In the days of Cornelius Bell, all twelve would have been filled, with a couple of spares provided in case of accident.

Now the time for the sixth Gift was approaching, and Darius's father was responsible for providing it. For months he had been telling Darius, Cyrus and everyone else that it was being prepared and would be a wonderful surprise – and he refused to say more. The entire city was trying to guess what it was, and hardly a week went by without one rumor or another being reported in the local newspaper. Darius couldn't talk to anyone without being questioned. He had had to make Oliver Roberts and Paul Klasky, his two best friends, promise to stop asking him, although that didn't stop them from dropping hints to see what Darius would say. The more his father repeated that the Gift was going to be a surprise, the more impatient people seemed to be to find out what it was. But if the surprise turned out to be that there was *no* surprise, it would be no laughing matter. There had to be a Gift. The terms of the Bell Grant were clear. Darius had never actually seen the Grant, but even he knew about them. If there was no Gift, the land and everything on it would revert to the council.

Darius found his brother in the Orbicularium, a small, circular room at the center of the House, with a round skylight as its only window. At some time in the past one of the Bells must have been a keen collector of optical instruments, and the Orbicularium contained them. Or their remains. As with every other collection of interesting artifacts in the House, once the Bell who had collected them had passed on, no one had looked after them, and successive generations of Bell children had been free to play with them as they pleased. Or to break them, to put it another way.

"I knew I'd find you here," said Darius.

When Cyrus wasn't in his room, and when he wanted to get away from people, the Orbicularium was usually the place he came to. He liked to tinker with the broken instruments, constructing new ones from the pieces.

"Aren't you clever," replied Cyrus. He was trying to extract a prism from inside a telescope with a long pair of tweezers.

"Did you mean what you said before?" asked Darius.

"What did I say?"

"That we don't have the money for the Gift."

Cyrus looked up. "Use your brains, Darius. Where would Papa get it? We don't even have money for a new car."

"Papa says it's a vintage car."

"It was a vintage car when I was your age. And it kept breaking down then as well."

"He says the Gift's a surprise."

Cyrus shook his head pityingly. "And I suppose you still believe in fairy stories, do you? There is no Gift, Darius. Don't you see? Papa hasn't got any surprise. There's nothing."

"How do you know?"

"Isn't it obvious? Believe me or not. It's up to you."

Cyrus turned back to the telescope. Darius picked up an old microscope that was on the table. "Maybe we could sell these and get the money."

Cyrus snorted. "You're such a waste of space. This is junk, Darius. Anything that was worth anything got sold a long time ago."

Darius put it down. "Will they really throw us out?"

"That's what the Grant says. No Gift, no House."

"This is bad," said Darius. "This is really bad!"

"Is it? The House is like the name, Darius. What does it mean? It happens to be Arbuthnot-Huntingdon-Castleton-Bell, but it could be any name. It could be Anderson. It could be Pellegrini. It's just a name."

"It's what it represents," said Darius.

"And what does it represent?" demanded Cyrus. "A family that used to be something and still thinks it is. Everyone knows that, everyone except Papa. If we really want the family name to mean something, Darius, it's up to us. You and me. No point expecting Papa to do anything about it. And how are we going to do that? Not by pretending we're still like we were, but by doing something new! That's why I'm going to be an engineer. I don't care about this house, Darius. Let it go. It's holding us back. I'm going to build new things, bridges and buildings and things that people will use, real things, things that will make a difference. That's how we'll be something again. Think about it. You should do that as well."

Darius did want to do that. When he was old enough to go to university, he wanted to learn to do something important. Maybe he would be a scientist or an architect. Or maybe an engineer, like Cyrus. But he wasn't sure if that meant he had to turn his back on everything that had happened before. Cyrus seemed almost to take a kind of pleasure in telling his father that everything that had happened before was irrelevant. The more it hurt his father, the more pleasure he seemed to take.

Darius didn't know why Cyrus did that. He admired his brother. Cyrus knew all kinds of things and built amazing models of buildings in his room, practicing to be an engineer. Darius wished that just once he could make Cyrus admire him in the same way. But all Cyrus ever seemed to do was call him a waste of space.

"Look at our names," said Cyrus. "Darius. Cyrus. Hector. Why? Because those are the names the Bells have always had. You were lucky, Darius. They almost called you Cornelius."

Darius grimaced.

"Cornelius," said Cyrus.

"Stop it."

"Corny! Little Corny!"

"Stop it!"

Cyrus laughed.

"Do you really not care about the House?" said Darius. He paused. "Robert …Cyrus. Do you really not care?"

Cyrus didn't reply.

Darius looked around the room. It was a wonderful room, in its own way. In its shape, with its skylight, it was like a giant eye, housing instruments for real eyes of human proportions.

"What will Papa do?"

"Who knows?" said Cyrus impatiently. "He can do anything. He can give them anything he wants. Yet he keeps talking about this big, amazing surprise he's going to give. It doesn't have to be anything big. The Grant doesn't say what it has to be or how much it has to be worth. It only says he has to give *something*. It's his choice. He could give them a dollar. He could give them a bunch of carrots from Mr. Fisher if he wanted."

"What's the problem, then?" said Darius.

"No problem, except for the fact that Papa could never do that because it would destroy the family honor. It has to be something big and amazing or the family honor will go. That's all that matters, Darius, remember? Family honor. The family name."

"So if he can't give something big, he'd prefer to lose the House?"

"Who knows? He hasn't told me." Cyrus glanced at his brother. "Let's see how brave you are, Darius. Why don't you ask him yourself?"

Chapter 4

Darius's father was in his writing room. This had once been a music room, and one of the earlier Bells had covered its walls with red leather in the belief that this would improve the quality of sound. But there was no sign of musical instruments in it now. There was a desk, and a long sofa, and one large armchair, in which Hector Bell sat when he found that he couldn't write and needed to think, which was often. He lay on the sofa when he found that he couldn't think and needed to sleep, which was even oftener. The room was on the second floor of the House, at one of the corners, with windows that looked out in two directions, so Hector Bell could gaze out over the estate that constituted the entire world about which he wrote his stories – or half of it, at least.

"Papa," said Darius.

Darius's father looked up with a start. He was sitting in his armchair, but his chin had sunk on his chest, and from the slow regularity of his breathing, it seemed very likely he should have been on the sofa instead.

"Papa," said Darius again. He came into the room.

Hector Bell blinked a couple of times, then smiled sheepishly. "What is it, Darius?"

Darius sat on the sofa. "Papa, I have a question."

"Questions are good," said Hector. "If we had no questions, we'd have no answers!"

Darius frowned for a moment, but decided this wasn't the moment to argue about that. Although surely the answers would still be there even if no one asked the questions...

"What is it, Darius?"

"I was going to ask you about the Gift."

"What about the Gift?"

"Is it true we don't have the money for it?"

Darius's father stared at him for a moment, then started to laugh.

It must be true, thought Darius.

"Nonsense, Darius! Nonsense, piffle and puff! What could ever make you think that?"

Darius glanced at his father doubtfully. Just looking around this room, he could find ten things that would make him think that, starting with the faded upholstery of the right arm of the chair on which his father was sitting, and ending with the tear in the upholstery of the left arm.

"We don't have as much as we might use, that's true," said his father. "But we have enough!"

"Enough for the Gift?" asked Darius.

"Enough," said his father. "Enough is enough."

"Cyrus told me we can give anything we want. We can just give a dollar."

Darius's father laughed.

"It's true, isn't it? The Grant says we can give anything we want."

"It doesn't matter what the Grant says, Darius. What matters is who we are. We're Bells! The Bell Gift isn't something you can buy for a dollar, it isn't something you can pick up in a shop. It's something unique, something magnificent, something outstanding, something with elegance, grandeur, monumentality, and yet … at its best, at its ideal, something with an exquisite delicacy of expression that stirs the deepest emotions in our hearts." Hector Bell paused, eyes closed, one hand on his chest, the other raised in the air. "That, Darius, is the Bell Gift!"

"But where's it going to come from?"

Hector's eyes opened. His hand fell. "I'm working on that."

"You mean you don't know?"

"That's not what I said. It's a surprise."

"Papa, I don't believe in fairy stories."

"Darius, your brother thinks he knows a lot more than he does. But Cyrus doesn't know everything. I have a plan."

Darius looked at his father doubtfully. It was true that Cyrus didn't know everything, of course, although he knew a lot. And it was also true that Cyrus never gave his father credit for anything. And yet sometimes his father seemed to Darius just like a child, a big, vulnerable child, more of a child than Darius was himself. When he said things like "I have a plan," for instance.

Darius didn't know who to believe.

"It's only a month away," he said eventually.

"A month?" Darius's father chuckled. "What's a month?"

A very short time, thought Darius.

"An eternity. An eon. An age."

"Thirty days, Papa."

"Thirty-one, in many cases. They say Rome wasn't built in a day. But a month? A month would have been enough."

"Papa!" cried Darius in exasperation. "If we don't give a Gift, we lose the House. Isn't that right? Would you rather lose the House than give a Gift that isn't worthy of our name?"

"What use is the House without the name?"

Darius stared at his father. Quite a lot of use. Somewhere to live, for a start.

Hector Bell chuckled again. "I'm joking, Darius. The Gift will be worthy of our name, *and* we'll keep the House."

"Papa, we could sell a part of it," said Darius. The estate was big. They could sell a part of it and use the money to provide the Gift.

"What part would you suggest?" asked his father.

Darius frowned. "The wood, I suppose," he said reluctantly. What else could they sell? The rest of the estate was being used by Mr. Fisher or the Deavers or somebody or other.

"Really? When I was your age, Darius, I used to love the wood. I'd go to the garden house. It was all overgrown. I used to pretend it was an ancient temple in the jungle, where human sacrifices had been made, and I'd go there with my friends and we'd see who could tell each other the scariest stories. Mine would sometimes go on for hours. My friends' stories were always much shorter." Hector Bell frowned, as if the thought had only just occurred to him. "Funny. I wonder why."

Darius didn't say anything.

"You should try going there some time," said his father. "You might enjoy it."

"I could live without it," murmured Darius.

"Well, I'll bear it in mind."

Darius nodded glumly.

"Darius," said his father, "listen to me. I'll get the money for the Gift. We won't have to sell the wood. If all else fails, Cousin Julius will help us. Why, only the other week I had a letter from him."

Darius nodded again. Cousin Julius was supposed to be fabulously wealthy, and ever since he was a little boy Darius had been hearing how Cousin Julius was going to do this or Cousin Julius was going to do that, or how Cousin Julius was coming to stay or at least drop in for a visit, yet on each occasion Cousin Julius and the things he was supposed to do somehow failed to materialize. Sometimes Darius wondered whether Cousin Julius wasn't just a figment of his father's imagination.

"Cyrus says you could just give a bunch of carrots from Mr. Fisher," he said quietly. "Cyrus says that would be enough."

"Your brother says a lot of things," said Darius's father.

"Like what?" said Darius's mother. She was standing in the doorway.

"Cyrus says we should give a bunch of Mr. Fisher's carrots as the Gift," said Darius. "If we don't have anything else, I don't see why we shouldn't."

"Darius," said his father, "we're not going to be giving a bunch of carrots. Are we, Micheline?"

Darius's mother smiled. "Of course not."

"There's nothing to worry about," said his father. "I told you. It's all planned. Now, don't you believe me?"

Darius looked at his father and then at his mother. "Really?"

His mother nodded.

"And you really think Cousin Julius will help?"

"If we need him to, of course he will," said Darius's father. "How could you doubt it? A generous man, a noble spirit, a prince among cousins, and yet … simple, unassuming, humble."

Darius's mother coughed.

"I'm not saying we do need him, by the way, but *if* we do." Darius's father smiled. "He's never let me down. You can tell that to your brother, Darius. See what he says then!"

"Come here," said his mother. She sat down beside Darius on the sofa and gave him a hug. Darius squirmed out of her arms. She laughed. "Now go on," she said. "Stop worrying."

Darius left. His mother got up and closed the door.

She turned back to Hector.

"He's worried," she said.

Darius's father smiled.

"It isn't funny, Hector."

"I know. He suggested that we sell the wood."

"He loves the wood!"

Hector nodded. "We can't sell it anyway. The Grant says we can't sell any of the land or we forfeit the whole estate."

"And you didn't tell him?"

Darius's father shrugged.

"Hector!"

"As long as he thinks we can sell it, he won't be worried."

Micheline sat down. She sighed. "Hector, what are we going to do?"

Hector was silent. His face, which was normally so cheerful, was suddenly troubled. "It has to be a Gift worthy of the name, Micheline."

"But it can be anything, Hector. That's what the Grant says. Cyrus is right."

"Don't tell me what Cyrus says. I've heard it already."

"You can give what you like. You can give a bunch of carrots."

Darius's father shook his head miserably.

"Some tomatoes, then."

"And wouldn't the mayor love to see me do that! He's just waiting to see it happen. He's just waiting to laugh in my face."

"What difference does it make if he laughs? Look at that council of his. They're no better than a flock of geese."

"I don't care about the council!" cried Darius's father. "I care about the name. This name, Micheline! Bell! I will not dishonor it." He looked at his wife with despair in his eyes. He almost whispered. "Micheline, I can't give some pathetic little Gift. People will think we're poor."

Darius's mother raised an eyebrow. She thought there were very few people in the town who didn't know that the Bells had no money, even if the family continued to live in the mansion. No one who ever saw them driving their old yellow car could be in any doubt. Yet if Hector wanted to believe no one knew how they really lived behind the fence of the Bell estate, she didn't have the heart to tell him otherwise.

"Micheline, the name is all we have. I'd prefer to give nothing than to lose that!"

"And would you prefer to lose the House? Where would we go, Hector?"

"Cyrus wouldn't mind," said Hector bitterly.

"Of course he would. Hector, deep down, he's a Bell just like you."

"Sometimes I wonder." Hector was silent. His expression grew even more troubled. Finally, he took a deep breath.

"Micheline," he said, "I have made a decision."

Darius's mother waited.

"There is only one thing I can give. One thing sufficiently exemplary, striking, ingenious, awe-inspiring, and yet … moving, mischievous, magical. One thing, Micheline. One that I already have, and it will cost us nothing." Hector Bell paused, a flicker of a smile on his lips.

"What?"

"My stories."

Micheline stared. "But you never…"

"True, I never planned to give them to the world. I had always hoped to keep them for ourselves, for the boys."

"You must keep them," whispered Micheline.

Hector shook his head. "I shall give them to the city. They will adorn the library, one volume after the next, preserved in a glass case. The Bell Opus! I never wrote them for profit, nor even for the world to read them, but so it must be. The library can publish them, and they'll have a never-ending gift from the sale of the books. They can create a scholarship with the money. The Bell Scholarship! Surely there could be no greater Gift than this. Two Gifts in one!"

"Hector," said Darius's mother. "That is too precious."

"Micheline, I must do it."

"Hector, you mustn't!" There was a note of panic in Micheline's voice. The world hadn't read Hector's short stories, but she had. She knew what people would think of them, although she had never had the heart to tell him. If her husband thought it would be a humiliation to the Bell name to be thought to be poor, it would be nothing like the humiliation he would suffer once people read his stories.

"Micheline, what greater gift can I give?"

"This is too much, Hector. The world isn't ready. Send some tomatoes. Or eggplant."

"I'll give the stories."

"No!" Micheline had actually shouted it. Hector looked at her in alarm. "Darling," she said, quietly, gently, "they are *too* precious. I couldn't bear to see them go. It would hurt too deeply."

Hector frowned in dismay. "I couldn't bear to hurt you, Micheline. That would be worse than anything."

"It might kill me, Hector. In fact, I'm sure it would."

"I would prefer to lose everything than you, Micheline. Everything!"

"Even the honor of the name?"

Hector got down dramatically on one knee. "Even the name, my love."

"Then I beg you, Hector, don't give the stories."

Darius's father was silent. At last he nodded. "I won't give them."

"Send some cucumbers," said Micheline. "Or walnuts."

"But I can't. The name, Micheline. The name is all."

"Then we must think of something else, Hector. But not the stories."

"Then what?"

"Carrots. Or celery."

41

Hector shook his head. He tried to get off his knee, then put out a hand for Micheline to help him up. Eventually he clambered back onto the sofa.

There was silence.

"Cousin Julius will help," said Hector at last. "He's never let me down."

"He's never had to do anything."

"I'm sure he'll help."

Micheline looked at her husband with a worried expression. "Hector, it's less than a month away."

Hector nodded. Suddenly he turned to his wife. "A month?" He laughed. "Think of everything that can happen in a month. Micheline, a month's an eternity!"

Chapter 5

Darius wasn't sure he really believed that Cousin Julius would come to the rescue, as his father had promised. After all, he wasn't sure he really believed that Cousin Julius even existed. Cyrus laughed at the suggestion. He had no more idea than Darius whether there really was such a person as Cousin Julius, but he didn't believe for a minute that he would solve the problem of the Gift. If he was going to do that, he would have done it already.

"Maybe Cousin Julius is going to turn up with something at the last minute," said Darius. "Maybe that's the surprise."

Cyrus rolled his eyes. "Darius, what a waste of space you are," he muttered under his breath.

They'd have to sell a chunk of the land from the estate. At least there was always that solution, thought Darius. He half expected to see a "Land for Sale" sign nailed up somewhere on the fence.

But he knew which part it would have to be. The next time he went to the jungle house, he had that feeling you have when you know you're going somewhere for the last time, or almost the last time. You find yourself spending all your time thinking about what it will be like when you can't go there any more, and none of your time actually enjoying being there.

He was with Oliver Roberts and Paul Klasky. They had been best friends since the first grade. Oliver was a tall, thoughtful boy whose clothes always seemed to lag an inch or two behind his rate of growth. Paul was smaller and never believed anything the first time, or the second time, or even the third time you told him, unless suddenly, for some reason, something did make him believe it, and then you could never convince him otherwise. He also had a habit of repeating the sayings he heard from his father, who was fond of proverbs, without necessarily bothering to make sure he understood what they meant first.

They stopped in the kitchen on their way out, as usual. Mrs. Simpson was just finishing a batch of carrot cakes which her husband was going to take to the cafes in town. She was putting a layer of creamy icing on the last of the cakes.

The three boys watched her intently as she laid the icing on with the blade of a palette knife, just like an artist at a canvas.

Then she stood back, hands on her hips, and surveyed the cakes on the bench. There were eight of them, and the air was heavy and warm with their newly baked scent.

But there was always extra, they knew. Mrs. Simpson never sent everything off to the cafes, no matter how many miniature ceramic jugs her husband wanted to buy. She took a ninth cake out from a cupboard and proceeded to cut three thick slices.

"Shall I pack them for you?" she said.

Darius nodded. So did the other two boys.

Mrs. Simpson produced a container and put the pieces inside.

Darius glanced at the ninth cake, which was now only two-thirds of the size it had been. Soon people would be taking slices out of the other eight cakes as well, he thought, and they would get smaller, and then there would be nothing left of them.

There was still some room in the container. Mrs. Simpson cut more of the cake and put it in.

Now the cake was even smaller.

"Mrs. Simpson," said Darius, "doesn't it ever worry you? You do all this work to make these cakes, and then people eat them and they all disappear."

"Why should it worry me?" asked Mrs. Simpson, closing the container. "That's what I make them for." She glanced at Paul and Oliver, and smiled. "I want them to disappear."

Paul and Oliver grinned.

"But then they're gone," said Darius, "and nothing's left from all that work. And you have to start all over again."

"You know what they say," said Paul. "You can't have your cake and eat it too." That was one of the sayings he had often heard from his father, although he couldn't say exactly what it meant, and neither could Darius or Oliver. After all, if you didn't have your cake, how *could* you eat it?

Mrs. Simpson glanced at Paul for a moment, and then gave a slight shrug. She didn't know what to make of Paul's sayings any more than the others did.

"I don't think it's quite right to say that nothing's left," she said to Darius. "People have the memory. They'll talk about a cake for years, you know, if it's special enough. Take the cake my Aunt Batty made for my Aunt Willie's wedding. Four layers, it had, each with icing of a different color, and pillars of rock candy between. She made flowers out of icing sugar and butter – roses, geraniums and rhododendrons, of all things! She colored them with syrup made from the petals of the flowers themselves. No one had ever seen rhododendrons made of icing sugar and butter before, nor since, I shouldn't think. We still talk about it, you know."

"Really?" said Paul.

"Oh, yes. Quite frequently. We're all serious cake-bakers in our family. A cake like that isn't easily forgotten. It was the first of its kind."

"Well, you know what they say," said Paul. "The early bird catches the worm."

Everyone looked at him for a moment.

"What about you, Oliver?" said Mrs. Simpson.

"I'm not a serious cake-baker," said Oliver. "Although I might consider it in the future."

Mrs. Simpson chuckled.

"It's still not the same as a thing someone can keep," said Darius.

"No, that's true," said Mrs. Simpson. "I suppose it's more of an experience. That's what you keep. The sight of the cake, the taste, the pleasure of eating it. The friends you ate it with. I don't see why that isn't as valuable as anything else. The perfect cake makes the perfect occasion."

Darius thought about it.

Mrs. Simpson handed the container to him. "Now off you go. I haven't time to stand around talking. I've got dinner to make yet!"

They headed out.

"Wait a minute," she called after them. "What about napkins?"

Napkins! They glanced at each other and laughed.

Outside, Marguerite waved at Darius as they went past the gardener's house. Paul sniggered and Darius elbowed him in the ribs. They went past the fishpond and headed into the wood. The growth in the wood was dense and tangled, but they knew their way through. They reached the overgrown clearing with the ancient, broken fountain. Ahead of them was the fallen log that led to the jungle house. One after the other, they walked along the log, making their way over the slippery, mossy wood. It was easy to fall off, and each of them had done it on occasion, tumbling into the undergrowth on one side or the other and coming up with scratches and bruises. It was the danger that made it fun. They shouted at each other as they crossed, yelling out anything they thought would make one of the others laugh or shout back or get distracted in some other way so he'd fall.

The house on the other side was like a big, empty shell. When you looked out, you could see the figure of the boy and girl on the fountain poking up out of the bushes, like two lost children who had turned to stone, and beyond them the trees of the wood. The best time was when it was close to evening, and the shadows under the trees began to darken, and the whole scene seemed like some eerie image out of a horror story, and you could imagine the ghosts of the vengeful dead stalking the wood. The fact that you knew you'd have to walk back through the wood in near-darkness just made everything even spookier. Sometimes they dared each other to keep staying and waited to see who'd be the first to say it was getting too dark and jump up to cross the log to go back. Paul Klasky, usually.

But it was light now, as they sat on the stone floor of the jungle house and ate their cake. The cake was still slightly warm, even after the walk to get there, and it couldn't have been better. He'd remember this cake, thought Darius, just as Mrs. Simpson had said. Then he thought that he'd remember it even more, because soon he might not be able to come to the jungle house. His father would sell this part of the estate to get money for the Gift, and then the jungle house would be gone, and the wood too, probably, because whoever bought it would cut down the trees so they could build on the land, and then there'd be normal houses here, and sidewalks, and streets, just as there were everywhere else outside the fence of the estate. And no one else would even know what had once been here, no one but him, and Oliver and Paul, and maybe after a while even they would forget. But he wouldn't.

He'd never forget. That was all he could think about now, sitting in the house with the two stone children poking up out of the overgrowth in front of him. He couldn't enjoy being here with his friends for thinking about the fact that soon he might never be able to come here again.

Yet Darius couldn't see any other solution to the difficulty of the Gift, not unless Cousin Julius turned out to be a real person and appeared one day with enough money to buy one, or not unless his father decided to give a bunch of carrots from Mr. Fisher. And each of those possibilities was equally unlikely. Other than that, Darius couldn't see what else could possibly happen to solve the problem.

Chapter 6

It struck at night, about a week later. Something crashed and Darius woke up. The bed was shaking. But almost as soon as Darius was aware of it, the shaking was over.

Darius lay very still, listening, waiting to see what was coming next. Had he dreamt the crash and the shaking, or had they really happened? He reached for the lamp that normally stood beside the bed. It was gone. He found it on the floor. Darius picked it up and turned on the light. Things had fallen off the chest of drawers in the corner. On the wall opposite the bed, a picture hook had come loose and the picture that had hung from it was on the floor, the glass in its frame smashed. Perhaps that was the noise that had woken him.

His door opened. Darius's mother looked in, wearing her dressing gown.

"Darius," she said, "are you all right?"

Darius nodded.

His brother appeared in the doorway as well, grinning. "Can you believe it? Right here. An earthquake!"

Darius's mother looked around. "It couldn't have been an earthquake."

"Of course it could," said Cyrus. "What else was it?"

It was an earthquake. A tiny one by most standards, but enough to give everyone in the town a fright. Things had shaken, windows had cracked, and one or two old, rotten trees had fallen over. No one was injured except for an old lady, a Mrs. Dempster, who had been sewing at the time, and the sewing machine had jumped and put a needle through her finger. Everyone agreed it was unfortunate, although there were some who said that if you were going to be sewing at three in the morning, which was when the quake struck, it was obvious you ran some risks.

Yet apparently the earthquake wasn't so unusual an event. At breakfast, Darius's father looked up from the newspaper in surprise. "It says here," he said, "that on average we have twenty quakes like this a year."

"I'm sure we don't, Mr. Bell," said Mrs. Simpson, who happened to be in the room at the time, bringing toast or eggs or some such thing. "I'm sure I'd remember."

"But apparently we do, Mrs. Simpson. There's a Professor

51

Heggarty who's a geologist at the university who says just that. Here, look." Darius's father showed the newspaper to Mrs. Simpson, who gazed down at it with a frown.

"It wouldn't surprise me," said Darius's brother. "They're just too small or deep for us to feel."

Darius's father looked at Cyrus in amazement. "Exactly! That's exactly what it says here. Most of the quakes are detectable only with the most sensitive equipment. Perhaps you should be a geologist, Cyrus. You seem to have a natural flair for the subject. You could be a gentleman-geologist, and study rocks as a hobby. The study of rocks as a gentleman-geologist is a perfectly respectable occupation for a Bell."

"I'm going to be an engineer," muttered Cyrus. "Not a geologist. And not a gentleman-engineer, either."

Darius chewed his toast. "Do you really think there are little earthquakes all the time?" he said to Cyrus.

His brother nodded. "Parts of the earth are always grinding against each other."

"Really? Even now?"

"Yes, even now."

Darius frowned. It seemed amazing that all the time, when he was walking around, the earth was grinding away under his feet, even if it was happening so far below him that he couldn't even feel it. In fact, that only made it more amazing.

"Why do they grind?" he asked.

"Because the tectonic plates are moving," replied Cyrus impatiently. "Everyone knows that."

Darius looked at his father, and his mother, and Mrs. Simpson. It didn't appear that they knew about it.

"Anyone with a *scientific* education," muttered Cyrus.

"Ah, that explains it," said Darius's father cheerfully. "I was beginning to think this is something I should have known about. I'm a literary man, of literary sensibilities. I have no scientific education whatsoever. Some may say that's a misfortune, a deficiency, an oversight, and yet … can it not also be a blessing, a privil –"

Darius's father stopped, which was something he rarely did unless interrupted by the occurrence of a most extraordinary event. And indeed, that was what seemed to have happened. A bell was chiming.

"It's the clock," he whispered.

Darius's mother looked at him in alarm.

Hector Bell's eyes went wide. The chimes went on. "The clock, Micheline! The clock!"

Darius's father jumped up, his napkin still tucked into the top of his dressing gown. He ran out of the house. Everyone followed him. Outside, Hector Bell stood in amazement, pointing up at the clock tower.

The last of the chimes had just died away.

The clock had pointed at twenty-three to nine ever since Darius could remember. Yet now it showed eleven o'clock. And even though the time was just after eight in the morning, it seemed to be nothing short of a miracle.

"That clock hasn't moved in forty-two years," said Hector,

shaking his head in disbelief.

"The earthquake must have loosened it," said Cyrus.

"So a scientist would say," replied Hector. "Yet to a man of literary sensibilities, Cyrus, the significance is altogether different."

Cyrus rolled his eyes.

"I wonder what else has happened," remarked Darius's father, with a strange enthusiasm in his voice. Darius wondered whether his father realized that even if an earthquake might start a rusted clock, its other effects were generally of a more damaging variety.

Hector Bell handed his napkin to Darius's mother. Then, still dressed in his dressing gown, he set off on a tour of inspection of the House. Darius went with him. So did Cyrus, acting as if he didn't really care what had happened to the House, muttering that it would be the best thing for all of them if it simply collapsed in a heap.

Since just about everything in Bell House was in need of repair to start with, all kinds of minor damage had taken place. Tiles had come off the roof, pipes had loosened. They found rooms where chunks of plaster had fallen off the ceiling, and rooms where windows had cracked. Picture frames had shaken loose and objects had tumbled off shelves. The stuffed head of an elk, which had been hunted by a long-dead Bell and hung on the wall above the first landing of the east staircase, now hung upside down, its huge antlers pointing at the floor. Hector Bell exclaimed about each new piece of damage with exuberance, as if they were on some sort of safari and each discovery was a sight to be treasured. In the green dining room, the wallpaper had peeled partially down the walls like long, wilting leaves. It was an interesting effect, thought Darius, and slightly spooky. His father gazed at it for a long time, and Darius suspected this would appear in one of his short stories. In fact, he suspected that very soon there would be a short story about an earthquake that took place in the middle of the night and miraculously started a long-silent clock, and that everything else they were seeing would appear in it as well. And he suspected that this story would be written long before any of these things were repaired.

But Darius's father didn't go any further in his inspection safari than the House. He didn't go out into the estate, relying on the others who lived and worked there to inform him if anything had happened. And they, of course, knew only about the parts of the estate that they used. If something had happened elsewhere in the grounds, no one would have known.

Chapter 7

Paul Klasky doubted the possibility that there were tiny earthquakes happening all the time.

"We'd feel them!" he said.

"They're too small and they happen too deep in the earth," replied Darius. "I told you, it was in the newspaper. There's a geologist called Professor Heggarty at the university who said it."

"You can't believe everything you read in the papers," said Paul, which was one of his father's favorite sayings.

Darius glanced at Oliver and rolled his eyes. He explained the facts to Paul again. Exceptionally sensitive instruments were required to detect the quakes. But they were certainly happening. The tectonic plates of the earth were shifting all the time.

"Tectonic plates?" Paul shook his head. "What are they? Have you ever seen them?"

"You can't see them."

"Well, I don't believe what I can't see with my own two eyes," said Paul, throwing in another saying from his father.

"Or what you can't feel with your own two feet, I suppose."

"It sounds possible to me," said Oliver. "I'm sure there are all kinds of things happening that we can't see and we can't feel."

"Yeah, like giant moles running around and making the earth shake, I suppose," said Paul. "I bet you'd believe that if Darius said he'd read it in the paper."

"No. Moles don't run. In fact, they have extremely short legs in relation to their body."

"How do you know?"

"I've seen one."

"What do they do, then?"

"Burrow."

"Same difference," said Paul.

They came to the pond. A car was parked nearby and Mr. Gardiner, the fishmonger, was standing on a small wooden pier that jutted into the water, gathering fish with a net. He saw the three boys and waved.

"Everyone all right at the House?" called the fishmonger

from the end of the pier. "No injuries the other day?"

Darius shook his head. Marguerite had told him that a few of Mr. Fisher's pots had fallen and smashed inside the gardener's potting shed, but he didn't think that counted. "What about you, Mr. Gardiner?" he called back. "Everything okay?"

"No one hurt, thank goodness." The fishmonger tapped his left shoulder with his right hand, which was an old fishmonger sign for luck. "An earthquake! Right here! Who would have thought it?" He tapped his shoulder again.

The boys went on. They came to the wood and took the familiar route through the trees until they came to the clearing.

Darius stopped.

Things had changed.

The old tree was still there, leading towards the jungle house, but it was broken under a second tree that lay across it. The second tree had also crashed on top of the jungle house itself. Or what had been the jungle house, because the roof had collapsed under the tree's weight. Most of the walls had collapsed as well, and lay as rubble in the undergrowth.

"It's smashed to pieces," said Oliver.

"Must have been the earthquake," said Paul.

Darius nodded. The house wasn't the only thing that had been damaged in the quake. The fountain had lifted and tilted, as if clawed out of the earth by a gigantic hand. The boy and the girl leaned at an angle in the air. Beneath them, the earth had opened in a deep, black gash.

Darius went towards the hole. He stopped at the edge and peered in.

Behind him, Oliver and Paul came closer.

Darius could see rock inside the hole. He put a foot in.

"Darius," said Paul from behind him, "do you think you should be doing this?"

The rock sloped downwards. Steadying himself, Darius descended carefully. Then there was a kind of ledge ahead of him. Darius stooped and went under the ledge, and then he could stand upright again. The only light came from the hole above him. Gradually, his eyes grew accustomed to the dark. He seemed to be standing in some kind of cavern. He took a few steps further in.

"Darius?"

It was Oliver, coming down behind him.

"I'll stay up here," said Paul. "Just in case anything happens."

"Darius, what can you see?" said Oliver.

"I don't know… It's dark…" Darius took another couple of steps forward. There was something ahead of him … something moving gently in the faint, faint light that came from behind him. He strained to see. A kind of slight, smooth movement. A ripple.

Oliver was beside him now. "Water?" he said.

"I think so," said Darius.

Paul's voice came from above. "Are you all right? Darius? Oliver? What's going on?"

"This must be where the fountain used to get its water

from," said Oliver.

Darius nodded. "Have you got a flashlight?"

"No."

"Paul?" Darius called out. "Have you got a flashlight?"

"Why would I have a flashlight?"

"Have you got one?"

"What do you want one for?"

Darius rolled his eyes. "Have you got one or not?"

"No. What's going on?"

Darius tried to see how far the water went, but it disappeared into blackness. It could have ended a few feet away, or hundreds of yards away, for all that he could see. It could have been an inch deep, or three feet. Or thirty feet.

There was another ripple, just the faintest suggestion of a movement in the darkness.

"Darius? Oliver? What's happening?"

"Darius," said Oliver, "it's too dangerous like this."

Still Darius stood, wishing he could see more. It occurred to him that no two people had ever stood here before, no two people had ever seen this cavern and the water that lapped gently within it. In all of history, he and Oliver were the first.

He bent down and put his hand into the water. It was cold.

"What's happening down there? Say something!"

"Something!" called out Darius.

"That's not funny."

"I thought it was," said Darius to Oliver. "What did you think?"

"Reasonably funny," said Oliver. "Not hysterical."

"What are you doing?"

It really was too dangerous to go any further, as Oliver had said. Maybe there was a way around the water, but if there was, it was too dark to see it.

Darius turned. He and Oliver scrambled up out of the hole.

Oddly enough, although they had gazed at the pool, straining to see how deep it was and how far it went, neither of them had given so much as a glance towards the roof of the cavern.

Chapter 8

When they got back to the house, a big purple car was standing in front of the steps to the front entrance. A driver was holding open one of the car doors, and a man was getting out. He was a short, round man with thick grey hair and he wore an expensive, beautifully-cut blue suit. It was far more expensive and better cut than the old flannel suit which Darius's father was wearing when he opened the door for him.

"That's the mayor!" whispered Paul.

Out of the car came a young assistant carrying a briefcase. He went up the steps behind the mayor. The driver got back in the car to wait.

Hector Bell saw his son standing on the other side of the

drive. "Darius!" he called out from the doorway. "There's someone I'd like you to meet."

Darius glanced at Paul and Oliver. "I've got to go."

Paul looked at his watch. "So do I," he said, although he didn't seem in any hurry, and he watched enviously as Darius walked to the house. Meeting the mayor wasn't something everyone got to do.

In the doorway, Hector Bell put his hand on Darius's shoulder. "Mr. Podcock," he said to the mayor, "I'd like to introduce my younger son. I don't believe you've met him before."

The mayor looked down.

"Darius, this is the mayor, Mr. Podcock."

"Hello, Mr. Podcock," said Darius, and he held out his hand.

The mayor stared at Darius's hand for a moment, and then touched it briefly, with the tips of his fingers, as if it was some kind of dirty rag.

Actually, it was quite dirty, after all the scrambling up and down inside the hole that had opened under the fountain. But it wasn't a rag.

"Shall we go inside?" said Darius's father. He stepped back from the door to allow the mayor and his assistant through.

They went into the yellow sitting room, where there was a very large yellow sofa in which relatively few of the springs were broken. If you knew what you were doing you could actually sit quite comfortably. There were a number of mustard-colored armchairs in the room as well, but it was harder to find a comfortable perch on these.

Darius's father indicated one of the armchairs to the mayor and another to his assistant. They sat down, and immediately got up as Darius's mother came in. Then they sat again, and Darius's parents sat on the sofa. Hector Bell settled Darius on the sofa between them.

The mayor shifted uncomfortably. Darius glanced at his father. Guests usually got to sit on the sofa. If Hector Bell had put the mayor in one of the armchairs, it wouldn't have been by accident.

"Everything all right, Mr. Podcock?" inquired Darius's mother.

The mayor squirmed again, then found a position and held it, back slightly twisted to the right, left shoulder slightly dipped, and both hands clasped around his knees.

He glanced at Darius and coughed meaningfully.

"Don't worry about my son, Mr. Podcock," said Darius's father. "He's a Bell, after all. I'm sure there's nothing you have to say that a Bell can't hear."

The mayor smiled, or grimaced, whether in agreement or pain it was difficult to say. "As you wish, Mr. Bell. I'll come straight to the point, then, shall I? The Bell Gift. That's what brings me here. It is due, as you know, in a little over a fortnight."

Darius's father was silent. So was his mother.

"Did you hear me, Mr. Bell?"

"You told me that I know it's due, Mr. Podcock. Since I do know, that's hardly something that requires comment."

Darius glanced at his father again. He was getting the feeling that the mayor and his father didn't like each other very much. And he was right. George Podcock was a self-made man, having accumulated a fortune in haberdashery and underwear. The Underpants King, he liked to call himself. He prided himself on his forthrightness and intolerance of nonsense. He had very little interest in or sympathy for the Bells – who had made nothing of themselves, as far as he could see, unlike himself – and thought this whole notion of a Bell Gift in exchange for a grand estate was just the kind of nonsense that shouldn't be tolerated. If he had been alive in the days of Cornelius Bell, he would have been one of those who voted to give him a small metal vase. If that.

And yet, as mayor, he had no choice but to deal with the Bells over the Gift. And since the Bells showed no sign of coming to him, he had to come to them, unpleasant as that was.

"May I ask, Mr. Bell," said the mayor, uttering the words as if each one of them left its own bitter taste in his mouth, "what the Gift will be?"

"At present," replied Darius's father, "that remains confidential."

"But it's only a fortnight away."

Darius's father nodded.

"You cannot tell me anything about what it's going to be?"

65

"That would spoil the surprise, Mr. Podcock," said Darius's mother.

"Madam," replied the mayor. "I would rather not be surprised."

"Then it's unfortunate you're not the one to give the Gift, isn't it?" she remarked.

The mayor stared at her. Then he squirmed again, shifting in the armchair until he found a moderately comfortable position, or at least until the broken spring that was needling him was pressing into a different part of his flesh.

"Your predecessors," he said, turning back to Darius's father, "all gave notice. This allowed the municipality to do the necessary preparatory work. For instance, when your father donated the stained glass windows for the council chamber, the council was given three months notice in order to ensure they could be installed on the very day they were given. Isn't that right, Borthwick?"

The assistant nodded. He opened the briefcase and removed a piece of paper. "Three months and two days, Mr. Podcock, to be precise."

"It's so tedious to be precise, don't you think?" said Darius's father.

"No, Mr. Bell," said the mayor sharply. "I like to be precise. I find it's very useful to be precise."

"But tedious," said Darius's father, stifling a yawn. "Awfully tedious."

The mayor didn't respond to that. He looked pointedly

around the room, at the faded yellow fabric of the sofa and the faded mustard fabric of the armchairs, and at the faded yellow wallpaper, still showing the water stains of a storm that had smashed through a window and drenched one of the walls more than fifteen years earlier. There was a mirror that had cracked during the earthquake, and the mayor suspected that were he to come back when the next Bell Gift was due, in another twenty-five years, the crack would still be there. George Podcock knew all about these Bells. He knew they had nothing but their name and their house, and the only reason they had the House was because of the decision made by the council to give it to them a hundred and twenty-five years earlier. A decision that he, personally, considered to be intolerable. Whenever he drove past Bell House and saw its clock tower from the road he felt a personal stab of outrage. No one would have been happier than he were Hector Bell to fail to turn up in two weeks with a Gift. In one fell swoop the Bells would lose both the things they cherished, House and name. Yet the most intolerable thing about the Grant was that they could turn up with just about anything and it would be enough. This "surprise" they supposedly had in store was probably some pathetic little trinket they were making themselves. From what he knew about them, they couldn't afford anything else, and from what he could see when he looked around now, they could barely afford that.

Yet with a pathetic little Gift they would lose the honor of the Bell name. That at least would be one consolation for him.

"Well, I'm sure it will be a stupendous gift," said Podcock pointedly. "Far more spectacular than any of the earlier ones. People have high expectations, Mr. Bell. Last time, when your father gave only eight windows instead of the full set of twelve, people were disappointed. If I was in your shoes, Mr. Bell, I wouldn't want to let them down."

"On the contrary, Mr. Podcock, I intend to amaze them."

"Indeed, Mr. Bell? How so? Perhaps you can tell."

"A surprise, Mr. Podcock. The amazement will be doubled."

"And yet if the surprise falls flat, the disappointment will be tripled."

"A Bell never falls flat, Mr. Podcock. Never has, never will. Simply doesn't know how."

"Nor would he want to, Mr. Bell. It would be awfully humiliating, don't you think?" The mayor smiled cruelly. His lip curled. "The family name would hardly be worth the paper it's written on. People would talk. People are cruel. A laughing stock, that's all the name would be."

Darius glanced at his father. Hector Bell flinched for an instant, but only for an instant, and then he recovered himself.

"Have no fear for the Bell name, Mr. Podcock."

"Oh, I have no fear for it, Mr. Bell. It's entirely in your hands, is it not? I merely ask you what you intend to give."

"Just wait and see. Wait, Mr. Podcock, and be amazed."

"Very well, Mr. Bell. I shall look forward to it. You can't imagine how much." He stood. "Borthwick, up!" he barked, as if to a dog.

The assistant scrambled to his feet.

Darius's father left the room with them to let them out.

Darius looked at his mother. "Is it really a surprise?" he asked. "Do we really have something?"

His mother didn't reply.

"Did you ever see such a blustering fool?" demanded Darius's father when he came back. "Nonsense, piffle and puff! He'll eat his words. How he'll eat them! With vinegar on top."

"Papa, it's only two weeks," said Darius. For the moment, he had forgotten all about the damage to the jungle house and the hole in the earth and the cavern he had discovered underground. This was much more important.

"Two weeks?" said Darius's father. He laughed. "Just think what can happen in two weeks. Darius, two weeks is an eternity!"

Chapter 9

Darius didn't have a flashlight, but he knew who did.

"You want to borrow it, do you?" said Mr. Bullwright, when Darius found him early the next morning, and one of the builder's bushy eyebrows rose, and he cocked his head, and from the way he said it, it was clear that he doubted very much that "borrow" was what Darius really meant.

"If you wouldn't mind," said Darius.

"And what if I do mind?"

"Well, I'd still like to borrow it, but I suppose you won't let me. I'd understand, Mr. Bullwright. It is your flashlight, after all."

Mr. Bullwright considered Darius's request. He was a

small, wiry man, but immensely strong. Darius had seen him lift piles of bricks and bundles of planks that would normally have required two men. Yet like many builders, he had a nervous disposition, and his bushy eyebrows were always dancing up and down in anxiety. He was always worried that some structure he had put up would suddenly fall down, and that everyone would blame him. Which would be only natural, of course.

"It's not that I doubt your honesty, Darius, it's only, a workman without his tools, well, that's not much better than tools without a workman, is it? What if I have to get into a dark space to repair a roof? Or what if I have to look up a chimney or down a flue?"

Darius nodded. He could see Mr. Bullwright's problem. "I suppose you only have one flashlight, don't you, Mr. Bullwright?"

"No, but what if the one I'm using fails?"

"I suppose you only have two."

"No."

"Three?"

"The thing is, Darius, I like to have spares. I like to have six of everything. Then I'm sure I'll never get caught short. If only I had seven flashlights, I'd be happy to lend you one."

Darius nodded. "How many times have you had to use the sixth flashlight, Mr. Bullwright?"

"Not often."

Darius waited.

"Well, never," said Mr. Bullwright sheepishly, "if you put it like that."

Darius didn't know how else to put it. "What about the fifth?"

The builder shrugged.

"The fourth?"

Mr. Bullwright didn't reply.

Darius didn't say anything more. Ten minutes later he walked away from Mr. Bullwright carrying a big red flashlight that was still in its packaging. And yet the builder watched Darius anxiously as he walked away, his eyebrows twitching, already feeling nervous as his spare flashlight – or his fifth spare flashlight, to be exact – was taken away.

Darius came to the pond. The fishmonger wasn't there today. As Darius passed, a fish leapt out of the water, flashed silver in the sunlight, and plunged back in again. Darius stopped. He wondered why fish did that. Curiosity, perhaps, to find out what the world was like above the surface. If you were swimming along all day you'd wonder what was up there, wouldn't you, what that big yellow thing was that was shining down on you, for example, or those dark things flying over the top of you, or the leafy green things that you could see waving their branches nearby. Although they'd look funny, as things above the surface did when you looked at them from inside a swimming pool, distorted by every wave and ripple. And yet you'd want to know, if you were a curious fish, and surely some fish had to be curious. In a whole pondful of them, there had to be one or two.

Another fish jumped out. Or perhaps it was the same one, getting a second look.

Darius kept going. He went into the wood, along the path he knew so well.

In the clearing, the ruins of the jungle house lay smashed under the great oak that had fallen. The fountain in front of it was lifted and turned, just as it had been when he was here with Paul and Oliver the previous day, and the hole in the ground gaped open.

For a moment, as he stood in front of the hole, Darius did wonder whether he should have told someone where he was going, or made sure someone had come with him. He didn't know what he would find down there when he turned the flashlight on, and there was no way of knowing whether the cavern, which had been ripped open by the earthquake, was stable. Perhaps it might collapse or close up behind him.

But he didn't go back. Clutching the flashlight in one hand, he stepped into the hole.

He stooped to get into the cavern and cautiously made his way into the darkness. When he got to the point he had reached the previous day, he stopped. In front of him, he could just make out a faint, wavy ripple of water.

He had the flashlight in his hand. His finger was on the button for the light. Yet he waited a moment longer. One last moment of mystery, one last moment in which the darkness held endless possibilities. When he pressed the button, he knew, whatever he found probably wasn't going to be anywhere near as interesting as he imagined.

He pressed.

Instantaneously, the water lit up. It danced, it glinted, it gleamed. There were flashes of light everywhere, as if the expanse in front of him wasn't water, but a carpet of jewels.

Darius looked questioningly at the flashlight in his hand. It was just a flashlight. He looked back at the glittering surface of the water. Then he glanced up.

Darius's mouth fell open. He stared at the roof of the cavern, utterly dazzled.

Chapter 10

Oliver and Paul walked impatiently with Darius. "What is it?" Paul kept demanding. "What do you want to show us? Is it the Gift? Is it somewhere here on the estate?"

"Paul," said Oliver, "he's holding a flashlight! It's obviously got to do with the hole in the ground."

"Really? Well, waste not, want not," snapped Paul. "I don't see why he can't tell us what it is."

Yet Darius didn't. He didn't want to spoil the surprise. They'd see soon enough, and he wanted them to see it just as he had, suddenly bursting into life at the switch of a flashlight. Anyway, he hardly knew how he could describe it.

He had called them both. Straight away. They had to

come. He was so excited by what he had seen that he hardly knew what to think. Wealth! Riches! But was it possible? Maybe he had imagined the whole thing. Maybe the image of what he had seen down there under the earth had made him a little bit crazy.

Yet what if his father was about to sell the wood? What if he already *had* sold it? There was no time to waste.

They reached the clearing. Darius went down into the hole first, then Oliver. Paul came down hesitantly behind them. One after the other, they stooped under the entrance to the cavern.

"Turn on the flashlight, Darius!" said Paul. "What are you waiting for?"

"You'll see."

Finally both Paul and Oliver were standing beside him in the darkness. The water rippled faintly in front of them.

"Are you ready?" said Darius. He pointed the flashlight towards the roof of the cavern and turned it on.

The roof burst into light. Shining veins of gold ran through the rock. Crystals twinkled like stars. Oliver and Paul stared. Their mouths dropped open. Darius ran his light over the roof, and the sharp-edged crystals in the rock flashed red and yellow and white. The veins of gold glowed like a glistening web.

Below the cavern, the water of the pool sparkled, reflecting light from the glittering rock.

"What do you think?" said Darius.

"Look at the gold," said Oliver. "And the jewels. What are

they? Rubies?"

Spikes and blocks and encrustations studded the roof. The largest blazed red in the light. The crystals were sharp-edged, some chunky and multi-faceted, some like wafers or dominoes, all clustered and agglomerated, some neatly stacked, some seemingly exploding out of each other and falling towards the pool. On one side of the cavern, a huge formation, scarlet red, hung from the roof and reached almost to the water. Each facet and edge sparkled as the light touched it.

Through the roof came a thin pipe. In the past it must have fed the fountain above. Someone had driven it down through the ground without any idea of the riches that lay beneath.

"Who knows how much more of this there is?" murmured Oliver.

Darius nodded. Who could tell how much more gold and rubies there might be? The earth all around might be full of them.

"It must be worth a fortune!"

That was exactly what Darius thought. With all the gold and the rubies in here, the problem of the Bell Gift wouldn't be any kind of a problem at all.

"On the other hand," said Paul. "You know what they say. All that glistens is not gold."

Darius looked at him. "What is it, then?"

Paul shrugged.

"Well, what does that mean?"

"I don't know. Don't blame me. It's just a saying!"

"It must mean something."

"Maybe there's stuff that looks like gold but really isn't."

Darius glanced at Oliver, then looked back at the roof. If there was anyone who would doubt that it was gold glittering in the light, Darius knew, it would be Paul. And yet, if there was such a saying… It must mean something.

"Did you make that up?" demanded Darius.

"What?"

"That saying. About not everything that glistens being gold."

"No."

"Who said it? Your father?"

Paul nodded.

Darius looked back at the roof. What if it wasn't gold? And what if the crystals weren't rubies? Suddenly it occurred to Darius that the minerals in the roof of the cavern – whatever they were – might not be worth anything at all. He couldn't tell his father about it if he wasn't sure. He couldn't get his father's hopes up, only to disappoint him.

"Maybe there's someone who can tell us," said Oliver. "An expert. Someone who knows about this kind of thing. Minerals and rocks."

"Where's Darius going to find someone who knows about minerals and rocks?" demanded Paul.

"I don't know," said Oliver. "It's just a thought."

"What point's a thought if you can't do anything about it?"

"I can do something about it," said Darius.

The other two boys looked at him.

Darius switched off the flashlight. The cavern fell back into darkness.

"Let's go."

"You stay out here," Darius said when they were back at the House. "I won't be long."

He went up to Cyrus's room. Cyrus was building a model of a bridge. He had recently decided that when he was an engineer he was going to concentrate on bridges, and he had pictures all over his room of famous bridges from around the world, single-span bridges, double-span bridges, girder bridges, truss bridges, arch bridges, suspension bridges and variants of bridges in between. Whenever Darius was prepared to listen, he would explain the engineering principles behind them. He could talk about bridges for hours. Darius thought it was a bit childish to build models, and had once said so to his brother, but Cyrus had corrected him sharply. These models weren't kids' models, he didn't build them for fun. They were constructed exactly to scale, which meant they had to follow the same engineering principles as the bridges themselves, and therefore they enabled him to learn how the principles were applied. That was the point of the models, and engineers themselves often built them for exactly that reason. Speaking of engineers, Cyrus also had a picture on his wall of a short man in heavy black clothes and a top hat with a cigar in his mouth, which looked as if it had been taken a hundred years earlier, or even more. The man's name was Isambard Kingdom Brunel, and Darius knew it because Cyrus had told him so, and he continued to tell him so even when Darius refused to believe that anyone could have a name like that. Kingdom? The Bells themselves had their fair share of peculiar names, but at least they didn't call themselves Kingdom, not even as a middle name. Yet Isambard Kingdom Brunel, according to Cyrus, had revolutionized the practice of engineering and had built the greatest bridges of his time. He had also built other things, railways and buildings and even ships. Isambard Kingdom Brunel was Cyrus's all-time engineering hero. Yet all that Darius could think about, whenever he looked at the short man in that picture, dressed in that ancient way and staring out at him with the stubby cigar in his mouth, was why his parents had decided to call him Kingdom.

Cyrus looked up when Darius came in. He was holding a tiny piece of the model that he was about to put in position.

"What?" said Cyrus. "Why are you just standing there like a waste of space?"

"Which bus goes to the university?" asked Darius.

"You're a bit young for that, aren't you?"

"Which bus?"

Cyrus put down the piece and looked at Darius with interest. "Who do you want to see?"

"No one."

"You can see no one here."

"Very funny," said Darius.

"What makes you think anyone at the university will want to see you?" demanded Cyrus. "You'll be wasting your time."

That, thought Darius, was something he would decide for himself. "I didn't say I wanted to see anyone."

"Then why do you want to go?"

"I just want to go."

"That's not a reason.

"It's private business."

"You're too young to have private business."

"Cyrus!" yelled Darius in frustration. "Just tell me how to get there."

Cyrus stared at him for a second. "Ask me properly."

Darius rolled his eyes. "Robert, which bus goes to the university?"

"You're still too young," said Cyrus, and he laughed.

"Cyrus! I'll smash up your model!"

"Will you?"

"Yes! Now tell me which bus goes there."

Cyrus considered him. "I like to see a bit of fire in a youngster," he said eventually, as if he was some kind of grizzled old-timer himself.

"Cyrus…" growled Darius.

"All right, ask me again."

Darius took a deep breath. He really would smash up the

model if this went on much longer. "Which bus, Robert?"

"The number six. You can get it from Heaper Street."

"Thanks. I don't know why you couldn't tell me at the start."

"There are lots of things you don't know," remarked Cyrus. "Anything else I can help you with?"

"Yes. Can you lend me the bus fare?"

Chapter 11

Oliver sat beside Darius on the bus. In the row behind
them, Paul was next to a lady who was carrying a tiny
Chihuahua dog in a shopping bag. Somehow Paul got into
an argument with her about goldfish. Darius and Oliver
listened, glancing at each other and grinning. Paul was always
getting into arguments, and he had no idea how it was that he
always found himself sitting next to people who were always
so wrong. He refused to believe it had anything to do with
the sayings he was always uttering. Darius didn't know how
many times he had told Paul that it might be a good idea if he
understood what they meant before he used them.

"But goldfish are pointless!" Paul said.

"They're beautiful," said the woman with the Chihuahua. "Isn't that enough?"

"Beautiful?" replied Paul in disbelief. "How can anyone think they're beautiful? Goldfish have horrible, bulgy eyes. Remember what they say, beauty is in the eye of the beholder."

The woman frowned. "I don't think you've quite got that right…"

"I've seen them! I've seen plenty of goldfish. They always have bulgy eyes. And besides, you know what they say. Beauty is only skin deep."

Darius glanced at Oliver and grinned.

The bus turned into Founders Square. The town hall rose on Darius's left, with its stained glass windows and its tower with the magnificent copper spire, topped with the bellringer weather vane high in the air. On his right, in the square itself, he could see the marble statue of his great-great-great-great-grandfather, Cornelius Bell, and on the other side of the square, the Bell Fountain. It seemed that everywhere he looked he could see a Bell Gift. As they passed, the clock in the tower began to chime, ringing out on the Bell Bell, as if it wasn't enough that Darius could see a Bell Gift wherever he looked, but had to hear one as well.

Behind him, Paul's argument had spread – as Paul's arguments often did – and a man sitting behind Paul had joined in. But Darius wasn't listening. The sight of the Bell Gifts all over the square and the sound of the Bell Bell ringing in his ears brought his thoughts back to what this journey was all about. He didn't know what he would do if the geologist said that the glitter in the cavern wasn't real gold. He didn't even want to think about it. It had to be real gold, and the rubies had to be real rubies, and they had to be worth enough for his father to donate a magnificent Bell Gift that would shut up that horrible Podcock of a mayor once and for all.

The bus swung out of Founders Square and into Overington Boulevard, which was lined with shops and apartment buildings that had once been the most elegant in the city. It crossed the river at Meckel's Bridge, chugged up the hill, and then swept down along Bossington Drive. By now the entire back half of the bus was in an uproar and Paul seemed to be arguing with five people at once, or six, if you counted the Chihuahua, which was barking at him from the shopping bag on the lady's lap. The bus screeched to a halt and the driver stood up, hands on hips, glaring down the length of the vehicle.

"What is going *on*?" he demanded.

There was silence. Paul smiled innocently at him.

"In twenty years of driving, I have never, ever, experienced such disorder!"

"They say a change is as good as a holiday," quipped Paul.

"What was that?" yelled the driver, and he marched down the bus. "What did you say?"

"He said a change is as good as a holiday," muttered the woman with the Chihuahua.

"Did you?" demanded the bus driver.

Paul nodded. "That's what my father says."

"Well, your father's not here, is he?" The driver glared at Paul. Outside, there was a blaring of horns from the cars lined up behind the bus, which had stopped in the middle of the road. But the driver seemed not to be aware of them. "If I hear one more word out of you, understand me, one more word, you're out of here. I'll throw you off myself."

"But I only –"

"Nothing!"

"But –"

"Go on!" said the driver. "Say it. One more word. Make my day."

He waited. Paul stared at him, not moving a muscle.

"And the same goes for the rest of you!" said the driver, glaring at the other passengers on the bus. Then he marched back up to the front, got in his seat, threw one last, long look down the vehicle, and started driving.

The rest of the journey was unusually quiet. Darius didn't think he could remember ever having been on such a silent bus. At each stop, people slunk off, not daring to look at the driver or even their fellow passengers. And when new people got on, they fell silent as well, as if there was something in the look the driver gave them, or in the way the passengers were sitting, or in the very air of the bus, that silenced them. So the vehicle headed on, with only the noise of the engine to be heard, like a ghost bus inhabited by some kind of human-looking spirits who lacked the power of speech.

At last they got to the university. The bus stopped. Darius

and Oliver got off.

Paul paused next to the driver. "Thanks for the ride," he said, and he ran down the steps before the driver could get out of his seat, much less get hold of him.

They went into the university. In front of them was a broad path, and in the distance, at the end of the path, rose a big, cylindrical building. All around them were other buildings, some larger, some smaller, with other paths and areas of lawn between them. Here and there people were walking, looking very busy and preoccupied, and there wasn't a single child. How peculiar, thought Darius, a place where you saw no children. It didn't seem natural. Even at school, which was a place for children, there were always a few adults.

The three boys stood for a moment, not knowing where to go next.

Then Darius saw a sign. It showed a map of the university with the buildings drawn as big brown blobs. Every blob had a number, and there was a list along the side of the map in which each number was given a name.

"We're here," said Paul, pointing at a red circle on the map that said: YOU ARE HERE.

Darius looked down the list at the side of the map. About a third of the way down he came to a name: Faculty of Earth Sciences, Mineralogy and Geology.

"Number twelve," said Oliver, who had found it as well.

Darius looked for blob number 12 on the map and found it. "Where are we again?" he said to Paul.

"Here!" said Paul.

Oliver grinned.

Darius traced his finger over the map. "We take the third left, and then the first right. Agreed?"

Oliver and Paul nodded.

"Let's go."

They headed down the long path towards the round building in the distance. People gave them curious looks. Then one lady stopped and asked them if they knew where they were going. She had long brown hair tied in a braid down her back, and was wearing a green cardigan.

"To the Faculty of Earth Sciences, Mineralogy and Geology," replied Darius.

"Although we're really only interested in Geology," said Oliver.

"Really? You look too young to be university students," said the lady, and for some reason, she laughed after she said it, as if it were some kind of incredibly funny joke.

Darius couldn't see what was so amusing. It was obvious they weren't university students. Saying that was about as funny as saying the sky was blue.

"And what do you want at the Faculty of Geology?" she asked.

"It's private business," said Darius.

"Really? What is it?"

"Private business," said Darius.

"I'm sure you can tell me."

No, I can't, thought Darius. It was *private business* What part of *private business*, he wondered, did the lady not understand?

The lady waited for a moment. Darius smiled at her.

"Well," said the lady, "let's find you a map and see if we can tell you how to get there."

"We already found a map," said Paul.

"I'm sure there's one near here. There are maps all over the campus. We're quite proud of that, you know, so nobody gets lost."

"We already found one," said Darius slowly, wondering whether the lady had trouble hearing. Maybe she was one of those adults who had trouble hearing only when it came to children. "We don't need another map."

"No, don't worry. I'm sure we can find you one."

Well, thought Darius, you couldn't have a conversation with someone who couldn't hear you. Not unless you used sign language, and somehow he didn't think that would have made much difference with this particular lady, even if he had known how to use sign language, which he didn't, and even if she had been able to understand it. "Thank you very much for your help," he said politely, and he started to walk away.

Oliver and Paul nodded at the lady, and ran after him.

The lady stared after them in surprise, wondering whether they had been too rude or merely too stupid to recognize that she was trying to help them. Both, she decided eventually, and when she went home that night she would tell her husband how rude and stupid children were nowadays, and that she feared for the future of the university if the students who were going to turn up there in another few years were going to be the grown-up versions of the children she had met that afternoon.

Darius, Oliver and Paul continued down the path. The third turning on the left was between a concrete building that was five storeys high and a long, low white structure. The sign in front of the white structure said Agnes Hilton Desert Plant Laboratory.

"I wonder who Agnes Hilton is," said Paul. "I've never heard of her."

"I'd say she's interested in plants," said Darius. "Desert plants, apparently."

"I can understand that," said Oliver.

"Really?"

"I like cactuses."

Darius stared at him. "This is amazing. First I discover that Agnes Hilton likes plants, and now I discover that Oliver likes cactuses. It's true about universities. You really learn a lot!"

"You know what they say," said Paul. "Travel improves the mind."

They tried to look into the windows of the Agnes Hilton Desert Plant Laboratory to see the desert plants that Agnes Hilton liked, but the windows had some kind of white backing and they couldn't see anything.

"That's not very thoughtful," said Paul.

"Maybe you have to make an appointment to see them," said Darius.

"I'd make an appointment," said Oliver.

"Do you want to see if you can?"

Oliver thought about it. But it was a long way to come to the university, and his family had cactuses at home, so in the end he didn't think it would be worth the effort.

They kept going. They turned right at the end of the Agnes Hilton Laboratory, and passed another building, and then the path ended at a square building that was three stories high and had a pair of glass doors at the entrance.

"This should be it," said Darius, and according to the sign, it was.

Inside, the lobby was deserted. At the foot of the stairs was a directory. Darius looked at the names. "Here it is. Professor D. Heggarty. Second floor, room 2.5."

They went up. On the second floor there was a long corridor with closed doors on either side. Each of the doors had a number. Darius knocked on 2.5. No answer. He knocked again. Then he tried the handle. The door was locked.

"Not good," murmured Oliver.

Darius went to the next door and knocked. No one answered, but a noise was coming from inside. Darius opened the door. It was a big room, with benches and laboratory equipment. There was only one person inside, a man who was standing at a kind of big glass box, wearing goggles and earmuffs, and using a machine to grind something in a pot.

"Excuse me," said Darius.

The man didn't respond.

"Excuse me!" Darius took a step into the room. Eventually he went right up to the man and tapped on his shoulders.

The man stopped grinding. He took off his earmuffs.

"Sorry to disturb you," said Darius. "Are you Professor Heggarty?"

The man smiled. "No, I'm one of Professor Heggarty's students. Have you tried the Professor's office? It's next door."

Darius nodded. "No one's there."

"Well, then I don't know where the Professor is."

"What were you doing?" asked Oliver.

"Grinding up some rock. That's what I seem to spend all my time doing, grinding up rock."

"Do you like it?"

"Not really. But someone has to do it. It's for experiments."

"Is it for experiments on gold?" asked Paul.

The man smiled. "No. Why do you ask that?"

"No reason," said Darius quickly, and he gave Paul a nudge in the ribs. "Do you know when Professor Heggarty will be back?"

The man shook his head. "Would you like to leave a message?"

"No," said Darius.

The man shrugged. "Up to you." He put the earmuffs

back on, turned on the grinder and went back to his work.

There was no one else on the second floor. The doors were locked.

"I'm going to wait," said Darius to Oliver and Paul. He sat down in front of Professor Heggarty's door. "You don't need to stay. This could take a while."

Oliver and Paul sat down as well.

The sound of grinding continued from the room next door. Every so often it stopped for a short time, and then started up again, as if the man inside had finished with one rock and had replaced it with another.

"I don't think you'd learn very much doing that," remarked Oliver. "Not after the first couple of rocks. It seems a strange way to learn."

"I'd prefer it to going to school," said Paul.

"But you'd be bored after a while."

"And what about school?" said Paul.

They all laughed at that.

The grinding continued.

"This is a funny place," said Darius eventually. He looked up and down the corridor. So many rooms. "Where is everybody?"

"Who knows?" said Oliver.

"Seems like a waste of space."

"Waste not, want not," said Paul.

Time went on.

"I'm hungry," said Paul.

"You should go," said Darius.

"What about you?"

"I've got to stay."

Oliver glanced at Paul. Paul shrugged. "A friend in need is a friend indeed."

They heard footsteps on the stairs. But the footsteps went past the second floor and kept going. More time went by. Whenever Darius looked around, he caught Paul watching him. Darius pretended not to notice. He knew what Paul wanted to ask, and Darius didn't want to have to tell him, for the hundredth time, that the Gift was going to be a surprise. Darius glanced at Oliver. Even Oliver was watching him the same way. Darius wished Professor Heggarty would hurry up and arrive.

They heard more footsteps. This time the door from the stairs opened and a woman came down the corridor. She stopped at the sight of the three children sitting on the floor.

"Can I help you?"

She looked quite young, and had short dark hair and was carrying a briefcase bulging with papers.

"We're waiting for Professor Heggarty," said Darius.

"And what do you want with Professor Heggarty?"

"It's private business."

"Of a geological nature," added Oliver.

"Really? Of a geological nature?"

Darius nodded.

"Well, perhaps if you can tell me a little more about it, I

can see if Professor Heggarty would be interested."

"It's about a geological discovery," said Darius. "That's all I can say. I'm sure the Professor will be interested."

"Oh," said the woman, "you're sure the Professor will be, are you?"

Darius nodded.

"And you can't tell me any more?"

"It's private business," said Paul. "It really is. You know what they say. You don't wash your dirty linen in public."

The woman stared at him for a moment, then turned back to Darius. "Well, if it's such a private matter, I suppose you really do need the Professor, don't you?"

Darius nodded. "We'll just wait, if that's all right."

"By all means," said the woman. "But I am going to have to ask you to move."

"Are we in your way?"

"You are if I'm going to get into my office."

Darius looked around at the door with the sign saying 2.5, and back at the woman in front of him, and jumped to his feet.

Professor Heggarty pulled a key out of her pocket, unlocked the door, and went inside.

Chapter 12

"I thought professors were old," said Darius. "I'm sorry."

The Professor didn't glance up from her desk, where she was taking papers out of her bag.

Darius was standing in the doorway. "Can I come in?"

"I'm very busy," said the Professor, taking yet more documents out of her bag. It seemed to contain an endless supply.

"I won't take much of your time."

"He'll speak quickly if he needs to," added Paul.

The Professor straightened up, hands on hips. "Come on, then. In you come."

"Can they come in as well?" asked Darius.

"If they must," said the Professor quickly.

"They must," said Paul, and he nudged Oliver to get inside.

The Professor sat down behind her desk. "Since you know who I am, perhaps you'd care to introduce yourselves."

"I'm Darius Bell," said Darius. "And this is Oliver Roberts and Paul Klasky."

"Pleased to meet you." The Professor leaned over the desk and shook hands with each of them. Then she sat down again. "You said you had made a geological discovery, Mr. Bell. Personally, I doubt it. Genuine geological discoveries are few and far between. Ask my students."

"Well, I discovered something," said Darius.

"Indeed. What is it?"

"I found it after the earthquake. That's when I heard about you, Professor, because you were in the paper."

"You're famous," added Paul.

The Professor's expression didn't change.

"Well, anyway, this is what I found." Darius proceeded to describe the hole that had opened up in the ground, and the cavern, and the glittering roof that he had discovered when he turned on the flashlight.

"So you think it's gold and rubies," said the Professor.

Darius shrugged. "I'm not an expert."

"Well, Mr. Bell, I have to tell you that I have no interest in gold and rubies. Mineralogically speaking, they're not particularly important, and if they're not mineralogically

97

important, why should I bother with them?"

"They're worth a lot," said Paul.

"Indeed. They've always been worth a lot, yet what good have they ever done? What good will more gold and more rubies bring to the world, Mr. Klasky? What do they do for anybody, after all, except create jealousy and greed? I wish they were worth nothing."

"But I really need someone to tell me if it's gold and rubies," said Darius.

"You know what they say, Professor," said Paul. "All that glistens is not gold."

"Very true, Mr. Klasky." The Professor turned to Oliver. "And you, Mr. Roberts? What's your opinion of all this?"

"I'd like to know what's there," said Oliver.

"Why?"

"I just would."

The Professor gazed at him for a moment. "That's the best reason I've heard so far."

"So you'll come?" asked Darius.

"No. I have no interest in gold and rubies, nor in disproving that's what they are. And even though you might think that nonetheless I should come and check this cavern for you, Mr. Bell, if you look at it from my side, you'd have to ask, why should I bother?"

"You wouldn't," said Paul. "I can see that."

Darius elbowed him in the ribs.

The Professor stood up. "I'm sorry I can't help you. I'm

just too busy." She opened the door. "Where is this, by the way?"

"At my house," said Darius.

Professor Heggarty smiled, as if now she didn't believe a word of it. "In your backyard, I suppose?"

"I suppose you could say that."

"Bell House doesn't exactly have a backyard," explained Oliver.

"Bell House?" The expression on the Professor's face changed. She closed the door. "Why didn't you say so?"

"You didn't ask," said Darius.

"He thought you might go stealing them for yourself," said Paul.

"I did not!" Darius elbowed Paul again.

The Professor sat down. She looked at Darius.

"You're one of the *Bells*, aren't you?"

Darius nodded.

"I should have realized it."

"I still don't see why it makes a difference," said Darius. "If you're not interested in gold and rubies, does it matter where they are?"

"I'm not interested in gold and rubies," said the Professor. "But I am interested in something else." She opened a drawer in her desk and pulled out a lump of reddish rock composed of sharp-edged, faceted crystals. "This is a sample of vanadinite, Mr. Bell. Have you heard of it?"

Darius shook his head.

The Professor put the lump of crystals in Darius's hand.

"Guess where that sample comes from."

"Poland?" said Paul, blurting out the first country that came into his mind.

"Your house, Mr. Bell. There are reports that when the house was built, chunks of rock like this occasionally appeared as they dug the foundations. Tell me, does this rock look like what you saw underground?"

Darius frowned.

"Is it worth a lot?" asked Paul excitedly.

"Nothing to speak of," said the Professor. "A geological collector might pay a few dollars perhaps, for an exceptionally nice sample. It's pretty to look at, if you shine a light on it, but so are a lot of minerals."

"Then why are you interested in it?" asked Oliver.

The Professor smiled. "To *know*, Mr. Roberts. This particular mineral, in its location and the shape it takes, can tell us a great deal about how the rock in a particular area was formed. In this case, the rock under our own city. And that is something I *am* interested in. Very interested in. Incidentally, you might find some other minerals with it. Wulfenite. Limonite."

"Limonite?" said Paul, grinning.

"Limonite," said the Professor sternly. She opened the drawer again and pulled out another couple of rocks. One was composed of flat orange crystals, the other yellowish-brown.

"I don't suppose they're worth anything either, are they?" asked Paul.

The Professor didn't even bother to answer. "Do these look familiar, Mr. Bell? Did you see them in the roof of the cavern?"

Darius gazed at them. "What about the gold?" he asked quietly.

"It could be gold – or it could be something else. It's not impossible for gold to be found with vanadinite. In fact, it's quite likely. But there are a number of other minerals that resemble gold superficially. In common terms, fool's gold, because it's easy to be fooled into thinking they're real gold when they're worth nothing. As Mr. Klasky says, all that glitters is not gold."

Paul beamed.

"Mr. Bell," said the Professor, "I have a proposition for you. Let's strike a deal. I'll come and look at this cavern of yours. I'll tell you if you've got rubies or vanadinite. I'll tell you if you've got gold or fool's gold. And in return, if it's vanadinite, you'll let me take some of it away in order to study it."

Paul narrowed his eyes. How did they *really* know vanadinite wasn't worth anything? They had only the Professor's word for it, and now she was suggesting that she could take some of it for free. Maybe she was pulling a fast one.

But Darius didn't hesitate. It was the most natural thing in the world for him to agree to the Professor's proposal. After all, everyone else who did any kind of work at Bell House got to take something with them. It was the only reason anyone did anything.

"It's a deal," he said.

"Excellent. I'll come tomorrow afternoon."

"What about today?"

"It's late."

"Doesn't matter," said Darius. "You could even come at night. It's dark underground anyway."

The Professor smiled. "Tomorrow, Darius. Now, let me have your phone number and I'll speak to your parents."

Darius shook his head. "I don't want them to know."

Professor Heggarty looked at him in surprise. "Well, I don't know if I can do that, Darius. It's your parents' property. I can't very well go in there without permission."

"She'd be trespassing," said Paul.

Darius elbowed him, not taking his eyes off Professor Heggarty. "You can't come if you tell them, Professor. And by the way, they don't know where this is. I'm the only one who can show you where to go."

Professor Heggarty hesitated. Darius saw her glance at the lump of vanadinite crystals on the table. He saw the look in her eyes.

"There's a lot of rock like that there, Professor," he said softly. "An awful lot of it. You could learn a lot. Isn't that right, Oliver?"

"That's right," said Oliver. "There's a lot just like it."

Darius watched the Professor. Eventually she looked up at him. "All right. Where do you want me to come to?"

"I'll meet you outside the main gate," said Darius. "There's a side gate we can use. I'll show you how to get there."

Chapter 13

It was vanadinite. Darius knew it the minute the Professor put the rock in his hand. The crystals were the same as the crystals he had seen in the cavern, the color, the shape, the pattern. And the other rocks she had shown him, the orange wulfenite and the yellow limonite, Darius wasn't sure he recognized them, but they were probably in the cavern as well. They would account for the flecks of orange and yellow between the red. And none of those minerals, not the vanadinite nor the wulfenite nor the limonite, was worth anything to speak of. Deep down, Darius knew that there were no rubies in the cavern. He didn't need Professor Heggarty to come to the House to tell him that.

But that still left the gold.

Even the Professor had said it might be real gold. All of Darius's hopes rested on that.

He lay awake that night, thinking about it. You could find gold with vanadinite, wasn't that what the Professor said? It was even quite likely. She wouldn't have said that unless the chances were high. Very high. Gold with vanadinite… Imagine if it was all gold, right there, under the fountain in front of the old jungle house! Suddenly Darius had a strange thought. It was as if Bell House itself had been keeping the gold safe, storing it away under the earth, making sure no one would squander it so it would be there at the moment when it was most needed, and now, when there was less than a fortnight left until the Bell Gift, when there was nothing left, nothing but carrots or cucumbers to give, that moment had arrived and the earth opened to yield up its treasure. As if it wasn't only the Bells who had to look after the House, but the House that looked after the Bells. It was a crazy idea, quite impossible, and yet it seemed quite wonderful to Darius as well.

His father would think it was wonderful. It was more of a literary idea than a scientific one. Cyrus would laugh at it, Darius knew, but his father would beam with pleasure. Darius would tell his father the idea, he thought, just after he told him about the gold, and his father would spend the next ten minutes enlarging it, embellishing it, expanding it, using three words when one would be enough, as only his father knew how to do. Darius began to imagine how he would tell his parents about the gold. Maybe he would just go straight into the yellow sitting room and tell them. He would warn them to sit down first, the way people did in movies, so they wouldn't faint from the shock. Darius smiled to himself. Just imagine the suspense! And then, when he told them...

Or maybe he wouldn't tell his parents in the yellow sitting room, but would take them to the jungle house without telling them why. He'd just tell them they had to come. Then they'd see the jungle house, and they'd naturally think he'd brought them out there to show how the structure had been crushed, and then he'd say, perhaps quite nonchalantly: "Look at that hole in the ground. I wonder what's down there." And he'd take them down into the cavern – they would take some persuading, but he wouldn't give up until they agreed to go down – and when they were standing by the edge of the pool he would switch on the flashlight, and suddenly they would see the gold, glittering and gleaming like a web around the vanadinite crystals. What a shock they'd get! Only he'd have to be careful, because if they fainted, as people did in the movies, they'd fall in the pool.

And after that... Darius didn't know exactly what would happen after that, but everything would be all right, and there would be enough money from the gold to provide a truly magnificent Bell Gift, and maybe even to fix all the things that needed to be repaired around the House, and for anything else his parents wanted to do. And they wouldn't have to sell any of the land either, not even the wood with the crushed jungle house in the clearing. But he would have to tell them quickly, before they sold it.

He wished the Professor had been able to come that day. Or the next morning. He was going to have to wait until the next afternoon and he hardly knew how he could bear to. But it had to be gold. Isn't that what the Professor had said? It was exceptionally likely. Of course it was gold. Gold with vanadinite. You always found them together.

Chapter 14

The Professor arrived outside the main gate in a big green jeep which was spattered with mud from geological expeditions. The student who had been grinding rocks in the laboratory was in the jeep with her. His name was Lawrence. Darius, Oliver and Paul got in the back of the car and Darius told the Professor to drive down Roebuck Street, which was the street that ran along one side of the Bell estate. There was a side gate in Roebuck Street that led into the wood. A terrific rattling and crunching came from the back of the car at every bump and when the Professor had stopped and opened the back door Darius saw that the noise had come from all the fragments of rock that were in there. Some were veined with crystal, some were studded with lumps. Some of the rocks were sharp-edged, some were round. They were black, blue, green, yellow, red, grey and just about any other shade you could imagine. There were various bits of equipment in the back of the car as well. The Professor took out a folding ladder and a strong canvas bag. Lawrence carried the ladder, the Professor carried the bag, and they set off after Darius, Oliver and Paul, through the side gate and into the undergrowth that led to the jungle house.

Darius stopped at the hole that the earthquake had opened in the ground.

"That's it," he said.

"Let's go," said the Professor, barely sparing a glance for the smashed ruin of the jungle house that stood nearby.

Darius led the way. Professor Heggarty and Lawrence came next.

"You have to bend down here," said Darius, after he had gone under the ledge at the opening of the cavern, but the Professor was already with him, as if going into holes in the ground and stooping under rock ledges and other such things were second nature to her.

A moment later, Lawrence was beside her.

Darius turned on his flashlight and the roof of the cavern came alive in glittering display. He watched the Professor. She gazed at the roof, but not in the way he had gazed at it, or as Oliver and Paul had gazed at it, but with a kind of sharp, serious, professional expertise.

"It's amazing, isn't it?" said Oliver.

The Professor didn't reply. She pulled a flashlight out of the canvas bag and turned it on. It was about ten times as powerful as Darius's flashlight and gave a very pure white light. She moved the beam across the roof of the cavern, continuing to examine it professionally, her glance moving systematically from spot to spot.

"What's that?" said the Professor, stopping her flashlight on the thin reed of a pipe that came through the roof of the cavern.

"There used to be a fountain above this," said Darius.

Professor Heggarty nodded. She moved the flashlight again. "See that formation?" she said to Lawrence. "And that one ... and that one ... and that one? They're all typical, absolutely typical for thermogenic vanadinite." The Professor glanced at Lawrence, who nodded. "Now that one ... that's extraordinary. I've never seen a formation of that size before. We'll have to get pictures of it. That's one for the books." The beam rested on the huge formation that came down almost to the water. The Professor examined it for a time, then moved the flashlight again. She let it rest on a cluster of sharp orange-yellow crystals, like a stack of squarish wafers that had been stuck up on the roof, almost obscured behind a big lump of red vanadinite crystals. "That's wulfenite. Again, typical. I'd have been extremely surprised if we hadn't found any here." She turned to Darius. "This is a perfect display of thermogenic vanadinite. Classic. It's like something out of a textbook."

Darius nodded. Paul and Oliver glanced at him in concern,

but Darius wasn't disappointed. He knew the crystals weren't rubies. He had known it ever since he'd held the sample of vanadinite in the Professor's office the previous day.

Out of her bag Professor Heggarty took a pair of full-length rubber boots, of the type that fishermen wear, and pulled them on over her trousers. Then she took out a small hammer with a sharp claw.

Lawrence had unfolded the ladder.

The Professor took the ladder and carefully stepped into the water. She kept going until the water was up to her knees, and she was under one of the vanadinite formations she had pointed out to Lawrence. It wasn't the largest example, but it was regular, and very red, and Darius could see that it was probably a very pure sample of the crystal. Lawrence shone the light while the Professor put the ladder down in the water and tested its stability. Then she climbed it. She knocked a couple of times at the crystal, the hammer flashing in the light. Then with the claw of the hammer she levered a crack in the rock, and a fist-sized lump of crystal came away in her hand.

The Professor came down from the ladder and brought the rock over to Darius.

"See," said Professor Heggarty, running the claw of the hammer along the edge of the crystal as Lawrence held the light over it, "ruby doesn't splinter like that. And the color's not quite right for ruby. We'll test it in the lab, but it's vanadinite. Everything about it says vanadinite." She looked up at the roof again. "Thermogenic vanadinite. This is fantastic! It tells us how the rock was formed, it gives us a good idea when. Not just here, but I suspect it will tell us about this whole layer, this whole stratum under the city. I never knew whether that piece I showed you yesterday really came from here. In fact, I doubted it. But with a deposit of this size... We're going to have to go back and rewrite most of the things we thought we knew about this area."

Darius looked at her doubtfully.

"This is fantastic! Darius, this has made my day. My year!"

"And it's not worth *anything*?" asked Paul.

"It's worth everything to me."

"But not to anyone else?"

The Professor shook her head. "Not a cent."

"What about the gold, Professor?" asked Darius.

"Oh, yes. Let's find out, shall we?"

The Professor handed the rock to Lawrence and went back into the pool. She moved the ladder a short distance and positioned it under a thick gold vein in the roof of the cavern. Lawrence shone the light on it.

The vein glittered as if the rock was ablaze. Then the Professor's hammer knocked at it, and levered at it, and a big segment came away.

The Professor came out of the water once more.

She put the rock on the ground. It was a piece of dark rock about six inches long, with a thumb-width streak of gold running across it. Lawrence shone the light on it. The

Professor crouched, raised her hammer, and brought it down hard.

The rock shattered into pieces. A section of the gold splintered into tiny, glittering grains.

"Fool's gold."

"I knew it! I –" Darius stopped. No, that wasn't what the Professor was meant to say. What had she said?

"I'm sorry, Darius. It's fool's gold."

Darius stared at her. He had been so sure, so confident. Professor Heggarty could have her vanadinite, but the gold, that had to be real gold.

"It's a sulphide of iron. Pretty to look at, but worth nothing."

"But don't you have to…" Darius frowned, he still couldn't believe what she had said. Everything he had thought about – telling his parents, bringing them down here, using the gold to pay for the Bell Gift – everything that he had looked forward to wasn't going to happen. "Shouldn't you test it in the lab or something?"

"We don't need to," said Lawrence. "Gold doesn't do that."

The Professor nodded. She hammered a piece of the rock again, and it shattered into more tiny grains. "This is fool's gold, Darius. Real gold won't smash. It's a metal."

"It's ductile," said Lawrence. "Hammer it, and it flattens. It stretches. It doesn't disintegrate into particles like that."

Darius looked at the roof of the cavern despairingly. "But there's so much of it. Maybe … maybe another part …

another piece."

"Geology has principles," said the Professor. "It has a logic, it's not random. The processes that create that kind of fool's gold don't leave real gold behind."

Darius gazed at the smashed fragments of glittering rock. It seemed so cruel. So unfair.

"And it's not worth anything?" said Paul.

"I'm afraid not," replied the Professor.

There was silence.

"Do you mind if I take a few more samples of the vanadinite?" asked Professor Heggarty.

Darius shrugged. Why not? He stared at the worthless grains of crushed rock glittering at his feet.

Darius sat with Paul and Oliver on the fallen log outside the jungle house. The sound of tapping and chiseling came from under the ground as the Professor and Lawrence continued to take samples from the cavern roof.

"What does she know?" said Paul. "She doesn't know anything. She's just a professor of geology."

"So who should we go to?" said Oliver. "A professor of music?"

Paul shrugged. "Well, you know what they say. A stitch in time saves nine." But he didn't say it very confidently, as if he knew himself that it didn't have anything to do with the situation. He just couldn't think of anything else to say.

"Darius," said Oliver. "Look at it this way. You haven't lost anything. It never was gold down there. You can't lose anything if you never even had it."

But he had had something, thought Darius. Hope. A dream. That's what he had lost. A scene in his mind of walking in and telling his parents what he had found and that everything was going to be all right. But dreams aren't real, he thought bitterly. The thing that he had lost wasn't real, no more real than the so-called gold. It was something he had made up for himself.

It was strange, thought Darius. That fool's gold, or iron sulphide as the Professor called it, glittered and gleamed just as much as real gold, and yet it was worth nothing, and yet real gold was worth so much. But people wanted real gold only because it looked so nice, and this looked just as nice. Yet it was worth nothing. Why was that? It didn't make sense. It seemed unfair. It hadn't seemed unfair to him when he had believed the roof of the cavern was full of real gold, but it seemed unfair to him now that he knew it wasn't.

Still the sound of chipping and hammering came from the cavern.

The Professor was pleased, thought Darius. At least that useless cavern had made someone happy. Not because of what it was worth. And not even because of how amazing it looked when the light went on. He didn't think the Professor had even noticed what it looked like or the effect created by that dazzling roof. All she cared about was the identification of the crystals that she found. The cavern could have been as ugly or as dull as anything, and she still would have been pleased as long it was vanadinite and iron sulphide in there instead of ruby and gold.

"Anyway," said Paul. "You've still got the Gift to look forward to."

Darius's head dropped.

"I don't suppose you could tell us what it –"

Oliver elbowed Paul in the ribs. "Darius," he said, "you're no worse off than you were yesterday. Really, you're not."

"That's right," said Paul. "You know what they say. If you pay Peter, you rob Paul."

Darius didn't reply, not even to ask Paul what on earth he meant by that one.

Besides, he knew that Paul was only trying to cheer him up. But there was nothing Paul could say that could lessen Darius's disappointment, nor anything Oliver could say. They didn't know the true cause of his dejection. It wasn't the rubies and gold that Darius had wanted, not for their own sake. Not wealth for the sake of having wealth. It was only because of the Gift that he really cared about it. If not for the Gift, he would have been the first to say that he hadn't lost anything, and that you can't feel sad at not having something you never really possessed.

And it wasn't even because of the Gift. Not as such. It was because of his father. Paul and Oliver didn't know about that, either. They didn't know how much Darius's father cared about the family name, how personally he took it, and they didn't know about the mayor, just waiting to see his father and the family name humiliated together.

"Darius," said Oliver, "you're really no worse off. You're really not."

Darius nodded.

"You know what they say," said Paul. "Nothing ventured, nothing gained."

Chapter 15

A month wasn't an eternity, as Darius's father had said, but it was a reasonable amount of time. Even a fortnight was quite long. But now there was only a week to go. And a week wasn't long. A week was short. A week was quick. A week was nothing.

Cyrus agreed.

"Well?" demanded Darius.

Cyrus shrugged, not even looking up from the model he was building. "Papa's in denial."

"What does that mean? He isn't denying we don't have anything valuable to give. He knows that perfectly well."

"He's denying what follows from that," replied Cyrus. "If

we have nothing valuable to give, than it follows that we have to give something that isn't valuable. Papa can't bring himself to admit that. It's too humiliating, so he keeps saying Cousin Julius will help."

"Won't he?"

Cyrus looked up from his model and raised an eyebrow. "Drowning men clutch at straws, Darius."

Darius frowned. That sounded like something Paul Klasky would say. And yet Darius understood exactly what Cyrus meant by it, which was more than you could say about the things Paul came out with.

Cyrus turned back to his model. It was a complicated construction which was apparently based on a famous suspension bridge that had recently been built across a valley in France. It had four columns and a total of eight long, curving spans. As Darius watched, Cyrus was threading steel wire over the top of one of the columns, which would then hold up the spans on either side.

Darius could see how the design of the bridge worked. It was amazingly clever – simple once you thought about it, which made it all the cleverer. Each pair of spans effectively held each other up, balancing one another via the steel wire that ran over the top of the column between them. Yet Cyrus had already told him that the design of this particular bridge was extraordinarily sensitive. The columns were exceptionally tall and slender in their proportions, and the curves of the spans unusually pronounced. For the bridge to stand, it required incredible accuracy of construction. If the balance of any two spans was just slightly wrong, or a column not perfectly straight, the forces pulling apart the structure would increase until they brought the whole thing down. And this was only a model, only about three feet long in total. To construct this bridge in reality, you had to get all of these things right at full scale.

"How long is that bridge really?" asked Darius.

"Slightly over two miles," replied Cyrus, frowning in concentration as he threaded the wire. "I'm using a scale of one to two thousand."

Two miles, thought Darius. Imagine getting all those things right – balance, strength, angles – with pieces that were not inches, but tens or even hundreds of feet in length. It was awesome. Darius could see why Cyrus wanted to be an engineer.

Cyrus started threading a second wire. Darius thought about what Cyrus had said. Was his father denying reality? He kept talking about Cousin Julius. But he didn't need Cousin Julius to help, even if Cousin Julius actually existed. There was still one last way.

"Papa can always sell some of the land," said Darius.

"No he can't," replied Cyrus.

Darius rolled his eyes. He supposed Cyrus was going to say his father wouldn't be able to bring himself to sell it, or it would damage the family honor if he did. Not that Darius wanted his father to do it, because he knew which part of the land he'd sell. But Darius didn't know if he even cared that much any more. After all, the jungle house was smashed, and the cavern he had discovered wasn't worth anything.

"He'll do it if he has to," said Darius. "What choice will he have?"

"None."

"So he'll do it."

"He can't, Darius." Cyrus looked up again. "He's not allowed to. Don't you know? The Grant won't let him do it. If he sells any of the land, we lose everything. Why do you think we haven't sold any already?"

Darius frowned. That was a good question. Why *hadn't* they sold any already? He wondered why that had never occurred to him.

Cyrus shook his head. "Why do you think we've ended up with all the Fishers and the Deavers and the Bullwrights and everyone else living here if we could have sold the land? If not for the Grant, everything would be gone now except for the House itself. Everything would have been sold a long time ago."

"Is that really true," said Darius, "that we can't sell any of the land?"

"I just told you."

"Then Papa doesn't know it."

"He knows it," said Cyrus. "Of course he knows it."

"No, he doesn't. He didn't tell me that when I said to him we could sell –"

"Believe me, Darius, he knows it. All right? He knows it."

Darius was silent. "Well, I'm glad, then," he said eventually.

"Are you?"

Yes, he was. He liked the Fishers and the Deavers and the Bullwrights. Life would have been much less interesting without them. And he didn't care when kids at school teased him that he lived on a farm or an apiary. They were just jealous. That's what his mother had told him ever since he had gone to school and started getting teased, and he believed it. And when he didn't believe it, he still didn't care.

Cyrus turned back to the model.

But if Cyrus was right about the Grant, there really was no way out. The realization hit him. All along, Darius had thought that selling some of the land was a last resort. Even now, when there was only a week to go, he had thought it would save them.

Cyrus looked up again. "What? Why are you just standing there like a waste of space?"

"You're serious, aren't you?"

"Of course I'm serious."

"There really is nothing Papa can do?"

"Not unless Cousin Julius appears," said Cyrus sardonically. He laughed.

"How can you joke about it?" demanded Darius. "Do you really want to lose the House?"

"Why not? It needs so much work it's falling apart. We

could move into something simpler and smaller and be much more comfortable."

"I don't want to move into something simpler and smaller and be much more comfortable!"

"Yes you do."

"No I don't!"

Darius didn't. He really didn't. He loved the House, even if it was falling apart. He loved the clock tower and the echo gallery and the dim, dusty rooms with broken furniture covered in sheets, and Mr. Fisher's vegetable fields and the pond and the jungle house, although that was smashed now, and he loved his own room, even if the paper was peeling in the corners and the crack down the wall under the window had gotten noticeably bigger since the earthquake. In fact, that just made him love it more.

Cyrus laughed.

"Don't!" Darius felt like smashing up his brother's model, even if the design was amazingly clever.

"Darius, we won't have to leave. All right? That's not going to happen. We can give anything. Papa knows that."

"But he won't do it. It'll be too humiliating."

"He'll survive."

"It'll ruin the family name."

"Good!" said Cyrus. "That'll be the best thing for us. Who cares about the name? It just makes things difficult. It gives people expectations. And look at what it does to Papa. All the time he has to pretend, as if we're still rich and powerful like the Bells once were. Well, we're not! The sooner Papa admits it, the happier he'll be. The happier we'll all be."

Darius gazed at his brother doubtfully.

"He could get a job. He could do something useful."

Darius gazed at him even more doubtfully.

"Darius, think how hard it must be for him. He spends his whole life worrying that people will find out the truth, that we don't have any money, that we aren't powerful, that Mr. Fisher isn't our gardener but a farmer good and proper. It'll be a relief for him. It'll be a relief for all of us."

"It'll kill him," said Darius quietly.

"That might be a relief as well."

"Very funny. It'll kill him if he has to give something small." Darius imagined his father standing in front of Mr. Podcock and the entire city council with a dollar bill in his hand, or a bunch of Mr. Fisher's carrots. The humiliation would be too much. "He'll never do it."

"He'll have to."

"But he won't. You said yourself he's in denial."

"That can't last forever. And the honor of the family name will be damaged even more if he doesn't do it. Remember, that's what Papa really cares about. What's worse, being poor or being a coward? If he gives nothing people will say the Bells are both. He'll realize that. He'll do it, Darius, he'll give something small, and it'll be the best thing he ever did."

"It'll kill him. He'll never be the same."

Cyrus shrugged. "We all have to change, don't we?"

Darius didn't reply to that. He gazed at Cyrus angrily. Sometimes Cyrus was harsh on other people, too harsh. This was their father they were talking about! Their father, who wrote stories no one wanted to read, and who never used one word when three would do, and who told tales of his youth that not even he believed any longer, and who seemed more of a child, Darius often felt, than he was himself.

Cyrus went back to his model.

Darius watched him unhappily. He didn't know how Cyrus could treat it so easily. Either their father stayed in denial, in which case they would lose the House, or he would be forced to go through a terrible public humiliation that would just about destroy him. Darius didn't think his father would be able to do it. And yet now he found himself having to hope that he would.

Darius felt horribly miserable. It was a kind of despair he had never known. He thought of the cavern near the jungle house. For a day he had believed the cavern contained the answer to the problem. He remembered his excitement, his hope, the way he had imagined telling his parents and how they would react, their disbelief, their joy. It was horribly painful now, to think of that.

The memory mocked him. What had happened to all the riches in the cavern? They had shattered under the blows of a geologist's hammer. They had turned into worthless lumps of flashy crystal and veins of false-gold rock.

Chapter 16

Overnight, the asparagus had come up. Mr. Fisher always said it was one of the miracles of nature, the sudden appearance out of the soil of plump, juicy shoots of asparagus, and it was hard to argue with him. Once it was up, asparagus had to be harvested the same day for the best freshness and flavor. Or so Mr. Fisher claimed. Impatient herbs, that's what Mr. Fisher called them. Once they decided to come up, up they came, and if you didn't get them at once they'd lose their flavor and tenderness, as if to spite you.

All the Fishers were out, the parents harvesting, Marguerite and Maurice bundling the asparagus shoots and placing them in baskets. The Fisher parents used a special flat blade to cut the asparagus shoot at its base. They worked quickly, and yet with extraordinary delicacy so as not to damage the shoots, carefully placing each one on the ground before moving on to the next. Marguerite and Maurice came along behind and bundled, handling the shoots with care amounting almost to reverence. At least Marguerite did. Maurice wasn't too reverential when no one was watching. He hated harvesting anything that he couldn't eat as he worked, and raw asparagus wasn't exactly the tastiest food. Nor was cooked asparagus, in Maurice's opinion. He hated that as well.

"First of the season, Master Bell!" called out Mr. Fisher cheerfully when he saw Darius. "There's no asparagus sweeter than the first of the season."

Darius nodded.

"You want to get Mr. Gardiner to give Mrs. Simpson a nice couple of trout from the pond for supper. Trout and asparagus! Mmmmm!"

Marguerite glanced at Darius and smiled.

"We might have that ourselves," said Mr. Fisher. "Eh, Sophia? Trout and asparagus tonight?"

"Why not, Edgar?" said Mrs. Fisher. "Let's have a treat."

"I'd rather have a mouthful of head lice," muttered Maurice, who disliked trout almost as much as he detested asparagus.

Mr. Fisher found it utterly perplexing that the son of a gardener – who was more a farmer than a gardener, in reality – could dislike asparagus, but his only answer to the problem was to feed more and more of the vegetable to his son, who consequently liked it less and less. "Sophia," he called out, "let's make sure we have an extra big serving for Maurice!"

Maurice grimaced and, behind his back, snapped a stick of asparagus in two.

"I'll help with the bundling, Mr. Fisher," said Darius.

"As long as you're careful, Master Bell."

"Of course he'll be careful, Edgar," said Mrs. Fisher. "What a thing to say!"

"No offense!" called out Mr. Fisher.

"None taken," replied Darius.

"Good," muttered Maurice, and he put down his basket and pushed his roll of bundling twine into Darius's hands and ran off before his father had a chance to stop him.

Mr. Fisher called after him a couple of times, but Maurice didn't come back. "Why *doesn't* he like asparagus?" he said to his wife. She shook her head and sighed, wondering less about Maurice's dislikes and more about why they bothered her husband so much.

"It looks like you're stuck here now, whether you like it or not," whispered Marguerite.

"Watch Marguerite," called out Mr. Fisher, bending to cut an asparagus. "Eight stalks to a bundle. Three twists of the twine – not too tight – and then tie a gentle knot. I know it's complicated, but Marguerite'll show you how."

"It's not complicated," whispered Marguerite. "Daddy just likes to think it is."

They bundled the asparagus, following Mr. and Mrs. Fisher and gathering up the stalks that the Fisher parents cut and laid carefully on the earth. The tips of the stalks were tender, delicate, and Darius worked carefully to avoid damaging them.

Marguerite let her parents get a few feet ahead.

"I saw you, you know," she whispered, "with that lady and that man."

For a moment, Darius didn't know what she meant.

"They came in a car, but you met them outside. And then you and Paul and Oliver got in."

Darius didn't say anything. He kept bundling.

"You took them to the side gate, didn't you?"

"How do you know?" whispered Darius. "We could have been going somewhere else."

"Roebuck Street's a dead end," whispered Marguerite. "The only thing down there is the side gate."

Mr. Fisher looked back. "No dawdling, children!" he called out. "This asparagus needs to get to market. The quicker the fresher!"

"Yes, Daddy," said Marguerite.

For a few minutes they bundled quietly.

"I didn't tell anyone," whispered Marguerite eventually.

Darius twirled a length of twine around a bundle of eight asparagus shoots, not too tightly, and not too loosely, just as Marguerite had shown him.

"Where were you taking her? That lady and the man who

was with her?"

"Nowhere," whispered Darius.

"Who was she?"

"She's a professor."

"Of what?"

"It doesn't matter."

"What did you want to show her?"

"Nothing."

"It must have been something."

Darius looked up. Marguerite was watching him, her hands automatically bundling.

"Careful or you'll do that too tight," said Darius.

"I won't. Don't change the subject. Did you find something? Is that what you wanted to show the Professor?"

Darius didn't reply.

"What was it?"

"Children! Please!" called out Mr. Fisher despairingly. "We're almost finished. Don't slow down now."

"Sorry, Daddy."

"Sorry, Mr. Fisher."

They bundled.

"You can show me," whispered Marguerite.

"It's nothing," said Darius.

"Then you can show me. It won't matter if it's nothing, will it?"

"It's not worth anything."

"I don't care. Is it a secret?"

Darius shrugged.

"I can keep a secret."

"I didn't say it was a secret," whispered Darius.

"Children! Please. *Please!* The asparagus!"

They bundled silently.

"I'm not saying I'll tell anyone about the Professor if you don't show me. It's not a threat, Darius. I'm not like that. You've got a right to your secrets like anybody else. But if it really doesn't matter, why won't you let me see?"

When they had finished, Mr. Fisher gave Darius half a dozen bundles of asparagus to take to Mrs. Simpson. Then he got in his car to take the crop to the market and Mrs. Fisher went with him to get a couple of trout for dinner. Darius and Marguerite watched them go.

Marguerite looked at him questioningly.

If she had threatened to tell, Darius wouldn't even have considered taking Marguerite to the cavern. But somehow, because she hadn't threatened, Darius found himself wondering why he shouldn't. There didn't seem to be any reason not to show her, after all. There weren't any jewels and gold to be protected.

"All right," he said. "I'll take you. Wait here. I'll be back."

Darius took the asparagus to Mrs. Simpson and went to get his flashlight. Then he came back for Marguerite and led her through the wood. He stopped at the edge of the clearing.

Marguerite stared. "What's happened here?"

"The earthquake," said Darius.

"Your little house is smashed. Where are you going to come with your friends?"

Darius looked at her in surprise.

Marguerite smiled mischievously. "Do you think I don't know where you go all the time with your friends?"

"Well, you didn't know this had happened, did you?"

Marguerite shook her head. "But that's not what you wanted to show the Professor, is it? A smashed house?"

"No," said Darius.

"So what's the secret?"

Darius pointed at the hole in the ground. "That is."

He led her down.

"Be careful here," he said, when they got to the ledge at the entrance to the cavern. "You'll have to bend a bit." They went in. "Stop. There's water there."

It was utterly black ahead of them.

"Is this it?" asked Marguerite.

Darius nodded.

"What's so special?"

He turned on the flashlight.

Marguerite gasped.

"It's pretty, isn't it?" said Darius.

Marguerite didn't reply.

Darius looked at her. Marguerite's eyes were wide with wonder. They reflected the glints and gleams of the cavern roof. She continued to gaze, her eyes moving from one spot to another and then back again, as if unable to take it in, to see enough of it.

Darius was reminded of what he had felt when he first switched on the flashlight in this cavern: the surprise, the awe, the disbelief at what was in front of him. So much had happened since then – there had been so much disappointment – that he seemed to have lost that feeling. And yet he felt it once again now, seeing the roof of the cavern not through his own eyes, but through Marguerite's, without any disappointment to cloud it.

"Darius, this is so beautiful!" Marguerite's eyes continued to wander around the cavern. "And look at the water. Look how it glitters as well." She bent down and ran her hand through the water at the edge of the pool, and ripples moved the reflected lights, as if the lights were not on the roof but floating on the surface. "This is so beautiful."

"Well, it's not worth anything," said Darius.

"What do you mean?"

"That professor was a professor of geology. She came to see what was in the roof. I thought it might be rubies and gold, but the crystals are something called vanadinite and limonite, and the gold is a kind of iron sulphide, not real gold."

"Did you think it was?" asked Marguerite.

"I hoped so. I hoped it would give us enough money for… Well, anyway, it's not worth anything. It's just of scientific interest." Darius turned the light off.

"Turn it on again."

Darius shook his head.

"Please, Darius."

Darius sighed. He handed Marguerite the flashlight.

Marguerite switched it on. The crystals in the cavern flashed and twinkled.

"How long has this been here?" she said.

"Forever, probably."

"No, when did you find it?"

"The earthquake opened it up."

"And you didn't know about it before then?"

"No. No idea."

"The earthquake..." murmured Marguerite. "Who would have thought there would be something so beautiful under the ground? Everyone should be able to see something like this, don't you think?"

Almost reluctantly, Darius gazed at the roof. A big cluster of sharp vanadinite crystals glittered orange and red in the beam of the flashlight. Despite himself, Darius smiled at the sight.

"I'm glad it wasn't rubies and gold," said Marguerite.

"Maybe I would have given you some as a present," said Darius. "Maybe you could have made a necklace."

"I don't care."

"But this is worthless, Marguerite!"

Marguerite shrugged. "If it was rubies and gold, you would have gotten someone to come and cut them out, wouldn't you?

And all of this would be gone." Marguerite paused, still gazing at the roof, smiling at its beauty. "I'd rather have this sight for a gift. I'd rather see it like this than have any number of rubies around my neck."

Chapter 17

From the top of the clock tower, Darius could see past the fence of the estate and into the streets beyond. That was one of the things that made it such a good place to think. When you got stuck, or whatever it was that you were thinking about seemed too hard, you could just watch the streets for a while, and you were sure to see something that caught your attention, kids playing football, or a father teaching his child to ride a bike, or people having an argument. Once he had seen a car accident. Fortunately it wasn't a very serious accident, at least not until the drivers got out. One of them slapped the other, and the other appeared to pinch the first one in return, and it went from there, although it was difficult to see exactly what was happening because it was so far away. Eventually the police turned up. Anyway, the point was, you were sure to see *something* when you looked out from the clock tower, and you'd find yourself forgetting about whatever you had gotten stuck thinking about, and then suddenly you'd remember again, but the funny thing was, you always seemed to have thought of something new while you'd been watching, something that unstuck your thought process, even though you hadn't been conscious of it at the time.

That was only one of the things that made it such a good place to think. Another one was that no one else ever came up to disturb you. And another was that a bird, or even two, often dropped in, and that was a further interesting distraction when your thinking got stuck. Although the clock tower wasn't quite as good a place to think as it had been. Ever since the earthquake, the clock had taken to striking at any old time. The hands moved, and stopped, and moved, and jumped, as if they had a mind of their own, and the chimes acted accordingly. The minute hand might sit on one minute to the hour for hours on end, and suddenly tick forward, and it was impossible to say why it had sat, or why it had finally moved. Sometimes the clock was silent for days, and sometimes it seemed to chime every ten minutes. If you were up there when the chimes started, the sound went right through you. Not only did it deafen you, but it vibrated right down into the very depth of your belly. So there was a bit of a risk in coming up here to think now, and you never knew when the chimes would suddenly start and give you a shock. But Darius didn't mind that. In fact, it made it a bit more interesting.

The clock hadn't chimed at all that day, as far as Darius knew, and he had no idea whether it was just about to. He gazed at the streets beyond the fence of the estate. He could see a lady on one of the roofs, hanging out washing on a clothesline. The sheets flapped in the breeze, white, bright, and the lady was like some kind of big black beetle, holding on to their corners and then letting them go. In fact, if you watched long enough, it began to seem that the lady wasn't in control of the sheets, but the sheets were in control of her, flicking her away from one to the next.

Then Darius found himself thinking about Marguerite again, which is what he had been thinking about when he caught sight of the lady on the roof. Or about what Marguerite had said in the cavern, to be more accurate. He remembered the way she had looked, gazing at the roof of the cavern, the awe and fascination in her face at that moment. And then she had said she was glad they had found no rubies and gold, even if he would have offered to give her some as a gift. Somehow the beauty of the cavern was precious, to Marguerite at least, even if the rock was worthless. Seeing it was gift enough.

And Marguerite wasn't the only one who valued it. Professor Heggarty had been delighted to find crystals of vanadinite instead of rubies. Not for their beauty, of course, but for scientific reasons. Darius doubted that Professor Heggarty ever stopped to think whether any kind of rock or crystal was beautiful, and all she ever thought about were the geological processes that had formed them. What use were rubies and gold, she had asked, compared with what she could learn from the presence of vanadinite on the Bell Estate? And she *had* learned from its presence – most of what people thought they knew about the formation of this area would need to be rewritten. So in a way, even if only for scientific reasons, the discovery of the crystals was like a gift to her as well.

The cavern was worth nothing, not in money. And yet both Marguerite and Professor Heggarty valued it in a way that money couldn't buy.

The woman was still hanging out the sheets. Darius had an idea in his mind. It had already started to take shape while he waited for Marguerite to finish looking at the cavern, and ever since then it had been growing and developing. Yet it seemed crazy. And yet it seemed as if it might actually be an exceptionally good idea. And yet it seemed totally crazy as well.

Genius or madness? It was one of the two. But who could tell him which it was?

Not the big beetle on the far-off roof, who had just hung out the last of her sheets. She picked up her washing basket and disappeared.

Darius climbed down from the clock tower. A minute later, the hands of the clock moved and seven chimes thundered out.

He met Paul and Oliver at the Strike First bowling alley. Paul thought of himself as a champion at bowling, ever since he had played one extraordinary game in which he scored six strikes for a total of 224. He had never come anywhere near that total again. Yet somehow he had convinced himself that this was his true standard, and that the hundreds of other games in which he scored seventy, or eighty, or ninety if he was lucky, were the flukes.

The bowling alley was packed. They had to wait almost an hour before they could get a lane. They played three games. Oliver won the first, Darius won the second, and Oliver won the third. Oliver had developed a worryingly accurate ball that speared in from the right side of the lane and had a habit of hitting almost any of the pins that were still standing from the first ball. He was getting really good. It was a concern.

"What a terrible day I had," muttered Paul, as they walked away from the lane.

Darius thought Paul had had a pretty good day, by his standards. At least there hadn't been too many gutter balls.

"So far below my normal standard. I can't understand it. Still, you know what they say. The exception proves the rule."

Darius glanced at Oliver and grinned.

"You did pretty well," said Paul suddenly, looking at Oliver.

Oliver shrugged.

"Luck!" said Paul, and he shook his head in disgust.

They went to the cafe and got a smoothie each. Paul kept muttering about his terrible luck as they sat down.

"I want to ask you something," said Darius suddenly.

Oliver and Paul looked at him.

He hesitated. "Not here. Are you finished?"

None of them were. They slurped down their smoothies.

"Let's go," said Darius.

"Where?" asked Oliver.

"You'll see."

"It's like the blind leading the blind," said Paul.

Darius took them to Founders Square. Huge flocks of pigeons were everywhere, gabbling and gobbling and flapping around. Some people were selling birdseed, and other people were buying it to feed to the pigeons. About a hundred of the birds were standing and pecking at each other all over the statue of Cornelius Bell.

"I don't understand why people think it's so great to feed birds here when they never feed them at home," said Oliver.

"You know what they say," said Paul. "What's good for the gander is good for the goose."

Darius opened his mouth to ask Paul what on earth had made him say that – but what was the point?

"What did you want to show us?" asked Oliver.

Darius pointed at the statue of his great-great-great-great-great-grandfather. "That," he said. "And that," he added, pointing at the fountain opposite it. "And that, and that." He turned to the town hall with its stained glass windows and the spire atop its tower. "They're all Bell Gifts."

"What's the next one going to be?" asked Paul eagerly. "Are you finally going to tell us?"

Darius shook his head.

"But it's due next week!"

"Paul," said Oliver, "we said we weren't going to ask him."

"But *he* brought it up!"

Oliver frowned. He turned to Darius. "Is that why you brought us here, to tell us what it is?"

"I wish I could," said Darius.

"What does that mean? You don't know what it is?"

"That's not quite it, either."

"Then what is it?" demanded Paul.

"Well, the thing is…" Darius drew a deep breath. "Can you keep a secret?"

"Of course we can!" said Paul.

"I mean *really*." Darius hesitated. "All right, I'll tell you. There is no Gift."

Paul and Oliver stared at him.

"We don't have one. I mean, my father hasn't got one."

"But don't you have to give one?" asked Paul.

"We do. But it could be anything. It could be a single dollar. It could be a bunch of carrots. It can be whatever we want."

Paul laughed. "You couldn't do that. Everyone expects it to be something absolutely magnif –" Oliver elbowed him in the ribs.

"That's exactly the problem," said Darius. "We don't have the money for anything absolutely magnificent, or absolutely anything, for that matter."

"But the mayor's been saying it's going to be stupendous. The best Gift yet."

"I know. He wants to make my father look bad. Everyone's expecting something extraordinary. Well, that's not going to happen."

"What is going to happen?" asked Oliver.

Darius shrugged. "Cyrus says my father's in denial. Maybe he is. We can just give a dollar. Really. Legally, that's more than enough."

"Why don't you just give ten cents, then?" said Paul.

Oliver elbowed him.

"Ow! Why do people keep *doing* that to me?"

"When I thought we'd found rubies and gold in the roof of that underground cavern," said Darius, "I thought the problem was solved. There would have been more than enough gold there to buy something magnificent for the sixth Gift."

"But it's worthless," said Paul, keeping an eye warily on Oliver's elbow.

"That's what I thought." Darius hesitated. "I've had an idea. Do you remember when you first saw the roof of that cavern? Do you remember the moment I switched on the flashlight?"

Paul and Oliver nodded.

"No, really think about it. Can you remember? That exact

moment, when you still didn't know what to expect and you just saw it. How did you feel? Tell me."

"Surprised," said Paul.

"Amazed," said Oliver.

"Gobsmacked," said Paul.

Oliver smiled. "Happy."

"Really?" said Darius.

"Yes. I don't know why. It made me happy."

"I guess it made me happy as well," said Paul. "It's funny, I don't know why it should."

Darius thought about that. He wouldn't have said it made him happy. He would have said it amazed him, flabbergasted him. Yet now that Oliver had said it, he agreed. It *had* made him happy, to see the roof gleaming, twinkling, and the pool below it glittering. And perhaps that was what he had seen in Marguerite's face as well. Happiness. Delight. Wonder. Pleasure.

The sight of it had that effect on everyone. Everyone except the Professor, of course. But as long as the cavern was worthless, Professor Heggarty was happy as well.

"What's this about?" asked Oliver.

"I've been thinking. Maybe that could be the Bell Gift."

Paul looked at Darius as if he had gone mad. "What are you talking about? How could it be the Gift?"

"That's the part I haven't worked out."

The part he had worked out was simple. If people got so much pleasure from going down into the darkness of the cavern and seeing the roof come alive with light and the water of the pool below it ripple and glitter – if that moment, when the light came on, made them smile with wonder, and if they gazed with delight at the twinkling red crystals and web of gleaming gold – then surely this sight itself was a gift worth giving. How many people smiled with wonder and gazed in delight at the statue of Cornelius Bell, or the Bell Fountain on the others side of Founders Square, or the stained glass windows in the town hall, or the spire atop its tower? No one. No one even noticed them, no one cared. Maybe architects occasionally gazed at the spire, but they had probably seen plenty of spires like it, and it wasn't wonder that they felt, but interest, at most. Yet everyone got delight from the cavern. Apart from Professor Heggarty – who must have seen hundreds of underground caves – who wouldn't?

If all those boring things in Founders Square counted as Gifts, surely the cavern and its pool was a greater gift than any of them.

"I don't understand," said Paul. "Do you want to move it here?" He looked at Oliver. "Could you do that?"

Oliver shrugged.

"Imagine if you *could* bring it here," said Darius. "Imagine if you could transport it and put it under the square."

"How?" demanded Paul.

"I don't know. But imagine if you did. Imagine if you could put it under here and people could go down and look at it."

"But how?"

"I don't know! But just imagine. What do you think? Would it be good? Would people like it, or would they think it was silly? Would they laugh at it?"

Paul and Oliver frowned.

"Well?"

"I'd like it," said Oliver. "I don't know about anyone else."

"I would too," said Paul. "It'd be better than old Cornelius Bell on his horse over there."

That's what Darius thought. It would be much better than Cornelius Bell.

"But how *would* you do it?" asked Oliver.

Darius shrugged.

"You know what they say," said Paul. "A bird in the hand is worth two in the bush."

"Paul…"

"What? All right, how about this one? Necessity is the mother of invention."

"And your mouth is the mother of nonsense," muttered Oliver in exasperation.

"That's not nice," said Paul.

"You know what they say," said Oliver. "Better to be honest than nice."

Paul looked at him in surprise. "Really? Is that a saying?"

"It is now," said Oliver.

"No, really?" asked Paul seriously. He didn't want to miss the chance of adding another saying to his collection. "Did you just make that up?"

"Does it matter?"

"Yes! Tell me. Did you or didn't you?"

Darius didn't find out. He wasn't listening. How *could* you do it? How could you move a thing like the cavern and put it under Founders Square? Who was to say it was even possible?

He thought about going back to Professor Heggarty, but he didn't think she'd be interested. Besides, it wasn't really a problem for a geologist. Was it? Darius thought about it. No, it was a problem for a different kind of expert altogether.

Chapter 18

"Are you sure it's an engineering problem?" said Cyrus.

Darius nodded. "I told you already. I'm sure."

Cyrus looked at him skeptically, as if he doubted that Darius would know an engineering problem if he tripped over one. "Why can't you tell me what it is now?"

"I can't just tell you. I have to show you."

Cyrus shook his head. He turned back to his model.

"Cyrus! I'm telling you, you've *got* to come and see this."

"I don't *have* to do anything."

"Cyrus!"

"You're such a waste of space."

"Cyrus! I mean it!"

Cyrus looked up at him again.

"Please, Cyrus. It's really important."

"And it's an engineering problem, is it? You promise?"

Darius nodded.

Cyrus considered for a moment. "Is it a complicated problem?"

"Yes."

"How complicated?"

"Very. You'll kick yourself if you don't find out more about it."

Cyrus considered again. "Then ask me properly."

Darius rolled his eyes. "Robert, I have an engineering problem and I'd like to show you."

Cyrus pretended to think about it a moment longer. Then he stood up. "All right, let's go."

Darius took him past Mr. Fisher's harvested asparagus beds.

"Where is this thing we're going to?" demanded Cyrus.

"You'll see," said Darius.

"Why have you got that flashlight?"

"We'll need it."

They went past the pond and Darius took the trail into the wood.

"I haven't been here for years," said Cyrus. "I used to come here all the time when I was your age. I used to come out to the jungle house. Is that where we're going?"

"Kind of," said Darius.

"Then why didn't you just say so?"

"You'll see."

They got to the clearing. Cyrus stared at the smashed jungle house.

"The earthquake did it," said Darius.

"That little earthquake?"

"That's not all it did." Darius pointed at the overturned fountain and the hole that had opened like a gash in the earth.

Cyrus glanced at him doubtfully.

Darius nodded. He held up the flashlight. "That's why I brought this."

Darius led the way down. He stopped at the edge of the pool. A moment later he switched on the flashlight, watching Cyrus's face as he did it. There it was! Even on Cyrus's face, that initial smile of wonder and surprise, and then that fascinated, searching gaze, roaming over the veins of gold in the roof and the brilliant flashes of crystal and the bobbing, glittering lights in the water below.

"You discovered this?" said Cyrus.

"It's vanadinite and fool's gold," said Darius.

"How do you know?"

"I asked a professor of geology to check it."

Cyrus glanced at Darius. "Where would you have found a professor of geology?"

"At the university."

Cyrus looked at his brother disbelievingly for a moment. Then he remembered. "So you did go, did you?"

Darius nodded.

"And you just went up to a professor? Just like that?"

"What else was I supposed to do?"

Cyrus shook his head in amazement. "And he agreed to come and look?"

"She," said Darius. "I had to persuade her, but then she agreed. Professor Heggarty, the one who was in the paper. She was very excited about vanadinite. By the way, there are also some limonite formations."

"Why?"

"Because you often find the two in the same location."

"No, why was she excited?"

Darius smiled. He knew that was what his brother had meant. But it wasn't often he got the chance to be the one telling Cyrus something that he didn't know. And it wasn't often that he saw his brother looking at him with an expression of amazement, and perhaps even of admiration. In fact, Darius didn't know if he had ever seen it.

"She says it will tell us a lot about the way the rock under the city was formed."

"Really?" said Cyrus.

Darius nodded.

"Well, isn't life full of surprises?" murmured Cyrus, gazing at Darius for another moment. Then he reached for the flashlight in Darius's hand and turned back to the roof, running the light across it.

Yes, thought Darius. Life was full of surprises. And the most surprising thing was that he suddenly had the feeling that this wouldn't be the last time he would tell Cyrus something that his brother didn't know. In fact, Darius had the feeling this was just the beginning, and as he got older, it would become quite a regular event. He had a feeling he was going to enjoy it.

"Vanadinite and lemonite?" said Cyrus.

"Limonite," said Darius. "Look, stop. That one there, that yellowish piece of rock."

Cyrus nodded. "And that's vanadinite?" he asked, moving his flashlight onto the huge cascading formation of crystals that reached almost to the water.

"That's right. That one's the biggest the Professor's ever seen. She's going to put a photo of it in a book. And over there, that's wulfenite. Those brownish crystals. But it's not worth anything. None of it's worth anything. It's all of purely scientific interest."

"And the gold?"

"Fool's gold. Iron sulphide. It shatters. It's not ductile."

Cyrus glanced at Darius for an instant. He nodded seriously and looked back at the roof.

"As I said, it isn't worth anything."

"But it's scientifically important," said Cyrus.

"True."

"Money isn't everything, Darius."

"I know that. But when I discovered this place, I was hoping we could use it to get the money for the Gift. If it was gold and rubies, I mean."

"Is that why you went to the Professor?"

"I wanted to find out."

Cyrus looked back at him. "Darius, I told you, it'll be better for everyone if Papa just gives them a dollar next Wednesday. That'll be enough for the Gift."

"But this is the Gift," said Darius.

Cyrus looked at him uncomprehendingly. "I thought you just said it wasn't worth anything."

"That's the point, Cyrus! It isn't worth anything, and yet it is. It's worth something! Everyone who comes in here smiles, and the way they look at it… It's as if they've never seen anything like it before. Oliver, and Paul, and Marguerite Fisher, they all say it's the most beautiful thing they've ever seen. The way it shines, the way the water glitters. Cyrus, compare it with the statue of Great-great-great-great-great-grandfather Cornelius. Who cares about that? Who even looks at it? Someone could take it away in the middle of the night and no one would miss it. I'm right, aren't I? No one would even notice."

"Except the pigeons."

"Exactly! Only the pigeons would care. This is much more beautiful than any of the other Gifts. This will actually give people some pleasure. That's worth something, isn't it?"

Cyrus looked back at the roof of the cavern. He ran the flashlight beam across the crystal formations.

"Just imagine if the Bells gave it to the town, Cyrus. What a Gift that would be! It would shut up old Podcock, that's for sure!"

Cyrus nodded.

"But how can we do it? Could we move it? Could we somehow take it from here and put it under Founders Square? That's an engineering problem, isn't it? What do you think?"

Cyrus ran the flashlight over the roof again, but this time the look on his face had changed. It was investigative, thoughtful. He craned his neck and moved the light, following it right back over their heads.

"I suppose it could be done," he said at last.

"How?"

"You'd excavate it from the top. When you'd moved the soil, you'd get to rock. That rock up there, but from the top. Then you'd cut through until you got into the cavern. You'd cut the rock into blocks."

"I wondered about that. Can that be done?"

"I don't see why not," said Cyrus. "You'd cut it and then you'd move the blocks, and when you'd dug out an area under the square, you'd reassemble them and cover them over again."

"And would it look as good as this when it was finished?"

"If you did it carefully."

"What about the pool?"

"You'd have to recreate the pool. You'd have to run water into it. That wouldn't be a problem."

"Then it can be done!" cried Darius excitedly. "I knew it!"

"But it'd be expensive."

"How expensive?" Darius almost whispered the words.

"I don't want to disappoint you, Darius…"

Cyrus already had disappointed him. His tone of voice alone was enough to tell Darius what was coming next.

"Think about it, Darius. It's a huge operation. Think about all the work involved, all the equipment you'd need, all the men who'd be needed to do it. Not only here, but excavating under the square as well. There's no way Papa could pay for this. Darius, if we had the money for that, we wouldn't need to do it. We could just go out and buy something else in the first place."

Darius stared at Cyrus for a moment. Then he put his head in his hands. He had been so close, and now the solution to the problem was suddenly as far away as ever. It was as if this cavern itself with its gleam and its glitter was mocking him. First it was jewels and gold that turned out to be crystals and iron sulphide, now it was work required to move it that turned out to be too expensive to do. Each time the cavern seemed to give him the answer, and each time, on closer inspection, the answer turned out to be false.

"Darius, it was a cool idea. And I'm impressed that you went and got a professor to identify the crystals in here. Really impressed. I'm not sure that even I would have had the nerve to do that."

Darius shrugged. At any other time, hearing that from Cyrus would have filled him with pride. But it didn't seem to matter now. Nothing seemed to matter in comparison with his disappointment.

"Darius, it'll be the best thing for Papa to give something

small. It'll free him. It'll free us all."

"It'll kill him," murmured Darius.

"No. Even if we could have moved all of this to Founders Square, it would still be better for Papa to give something small. And other people can still come and see this place. It's not as if they can't. It just won't be the Gift, that's all. Papa will give a dollar, or some vegetables, and in the meantime, this is still here, it's just as beautiful, and people can –"

"We don't have to move it," murmured Darius. Suddenly he laughed. "Cyrus, we don't have to move it! Why are we even worried about that?"

"I thought that was the engineering problem you wanted to ask me about."

"It's not a problem."

"What do you mean?"

"Nothing." Darius laughed again. "There is no problem. Absolutely none!"

"I don't understand."

"You don't have to."

"Darius, what's this about?"

"The Gift! What do you think it's about? The Gift. Right here."

Cyrus looked at him closely. Then he shook his head. "Darius, I've got no idea what you're talking about. You're crazy."

Darius grinned. "Am I? Maybe I am!"

Chapter 19

The cavern wasn't ready as it was. A number of things had to be done. Some kind of railing had to be put up, for instance, at the edge of the pool, to make sure no one fell in the water by mistake. The loose stones on the slope down from the hole needed to be cleared so no one would slip. A sign was required at the entrance to the cavern saying "WATCH YOUR HEAD." And outside, the overgrowth needed to be cleared along the trail that led from the side gate to the jungle house.

But all of that could be done, Darius knew. It was just a matter of persuading the right people to help. And of keeping everything quiet until it was ready. Darius knew exactly when he was going to tell his parents, and exactly what he was going to say. He had it all planned.

He found Mr. Ostrovich, the carpenter who was allowed to chop down three of the great oaks on the Bell estate each year, coming out of the wood, where he had just marked a tree that he was going to fell. Darius asked him if he could prepare a barrier. He was a carpenter, said Mr. Ostrovich. Of course he could make a barrier! But he was very busy, and besides, requests for work should really come from Darius's parents. So Darius asked if Mr. Ostrovich could keep a secret. At this, Mr. Ostrovich smiled. Like most carpenters, Mr. Ostrovich loved secrets. Darius took him to the glitter pool and switched on the flashlight.

Mr. Ostrovich gazed in amazement. "For this," he said, "I'll make you a barrier."

"Here," said Darius, pointing along the edge of the pool.

Mr. Ostrovich pulled his tape measure out of his overalls. He paced along a length of the pool. "This long?"

"Maybe a bit longer," said Darius. "There'll be a lot of people."

Mr. Ostrovich paced further and glanced questioningly at Darius, who nodded. He read the length off his tape measure and wrote a number down in a little notebook with a stub of pencil that he extracted from his overalls. Then he measured the distance back to the rock at each end of the length that he had marked, and he wrote those figures as well. Finally he held his hand up at about waist height. "Up to here?" he said. Darius nodded, and Mr. Ostrovich measured the height and wrote that down as well.

He put the notebook away. "I can have it for you by two weeks from Thursday."

"How about this Monday?" said Darius.

"Does it make a difference?"

Darius nodded.

"I don't suppose you're going to tell me why."

"I will, Mr. Ostrovich. Only not yet."

The carpenter nodded. "Monday it is!"

"And you won't tell anyone? And only you'll come out here, none of your assistants?"

"Darius Bell, I've already told you that. What Ostrovich says, Ostrovich does."

"Sorry, Mr. Ostrovich."

The carpenter looked back at the sparkling roof of the cavern. "Other people will see this, eh? Once the barrier is in place?"

"Yes."

"Lots of people?"

"Yes."

"Good. Then perhaps we should have a handrail as well, on the way down, so people don't fall."

"Could you do that as well? Really?"

"I could, and I will!"

Next, it was Mr. Bullwright.

"I was wondering where you'd got to with my flashlight," said the builder, folding his arms. "You've finally decided to bring it back, have you?"

"Not exactly," said Darius.

The builder's bushy eyebrows rose. "You're *not* bringing it back?"

"I will."

"When?"

"Soon."

Mr. Bullwright shook his head, a worried expression on his face.

"Have you used any of the four spares, Mr. Bullwright?"

The builder didn't reply.

"I will bring it back, Mr. Bullwright. Honestly, I will. But there's something else I'd like to ask you first."

Mr. Bullwright folded his arms again, and the look on his face wasn't encouraging.

It changed when he saw the roof of the cavern come alive in the light from his flashlight. His eyebrows went high, higher than Darius had ever seen them before.

"So this is what you wanted the flashlight for, is it?" he murmured, gazing at the ceiling with a smile on his lips.

"I want everyone else to see it, Mr. Bullwright. Mr. Ostrovich is building a barrier. It'll go at the edge of the pool so no one can fall in. And he's going to put a handrail in on the way down so people don't fall."

"Good idea," said Mr. Bullwright. "What can I do?"

"The top is a bit dangerous. Maybe we could put a little wall around the edge of the hole with a gap for the entrance, so people will know exactly where to go in. Not a big wall. It doesn't have to be very high. Just so people know where they should go."

"Three feet high?"

"I'm sure that would be enough."

The builder went out of the cavern, ducking under the ledge at the entrance. He looked thoughtfully up the slope that led to the outside. "We can do better than that, Darius. If Ostrovich is putting in a handrail, what if I cut some steps in the rock?"

"Could you?"

"Why not? They won't be perfect, but they'll be good enough."

"That sounds great!"

"And I could put some lights in."

Darius stared at the builder.

"Not too bright, eh? A few lights pointing up at the roof, to bring out the sparkles."

"That would be amazing, Mr. Bullwright! Can you really do that?"

The builder shrugged. "I'll run a cable from the nearest switching point."

"But you have to keep it secret, Mr. Bullwright."

Mr. Bullwright's faced changed. One eyebrow came down, followed by the other. As much as Mr. Ostrovich liked secrets, Mr. Bullwright distrusted them. He was a builder, after all, while Ostrovich was a carpenter.

"It's a surprise. Not even my parents can know."

Mr. Bullwright looked at Darius doubtfully. "I'm not much of a one for secrets," he muttered. "If you can't do something up front and out in the open, then you shouldn't be doing it at all."

"I agree," said Darius. "But it's only for a few days, Mr. Bullwright. Just until it's done."

"I don't know, Darius."

"Please… It's just so everyone will be able to see it."

"And it has to be done in secret, does it? Is that really important?"

Darius nodded. "It really is, Mr. Bullwright."

Mr. Bullwright sighed. "All right then. It goes against my nature but… I'll do it. Now, as for timing, I can get it done five weeks from Friday. Is that soon enough?"

"I was hoping we could get it done by Monday."

"Monday?" cried the builder, and he laughed. "You must be joking."

"Really?"

"You're serious, aren't you?"

Darius nodded.

"And I suppose that's important as well, is it? That it's done by Monday?"

Darius nodded. "Very important, Mr. Bullwright. If we can't get it done by Monday, it's not worth doing at all."

The builder looked at him doubtfully.

"Really, Mr. Bullwright. I'm not exaggerating."

Mr. Bullwright pulled a notebook out of his overalls and quickly leafed through it, forwards, backwards, then forwards again. At last he sighed, a deep, heavy sigh, as if what he was about to do was against every principle he held dear. "All right, Monday it is. I was meant to be starting an extension for Mr. and Mrs. Letsis in Overton Street, but I can always put it off a few days."

"Oh. I don't mean to –"

"It doesn't matter," said Mr. Bullwright. "I've already put it off three times. They'd probably get the shock of their life if I actually turned up when I said I would."

"But –"

"Don't worry. People expect it from builders. If you turn up to do anything before you've delayed it five times, people get suspicious. They think you haven't got enough work, so you can't be any good."

"So does that mean you're going to delay this as well?" said Darius. "Because it has to be done by Monday, and if you're going to delay it, Mr. Bullwright, you'd better tell me now, because I'll have to find someone else –"

"Monday I said, and Monday it'll be." The builder began writing in his notebook. "What I say I'll do, I'll do."

"But you just said you always delay at least five times and then –"

Darius stopped. Mr. Bullwright had looked up from his notebook. One of his eyebrows rose. "Monday," he said, and he watched Darius a moment longer, then finished writing the

162

note in his book.

Next, it was Mr. Fisher. Marguerite came along with Darius to find her father.

"We just want to clear the undergrowth near the side gate on Roebuck Street," Darius said.

"Why do you want to do that?" asked Mr. Fisher.

"It's overgrown."

"Leave it to me," said the gardener, "I'll get to it when I get a chance."

"But we just need a few tools, Mr. Fisher."

"What kind of tools?"

"Tools to cut things down," said Darius, thinking of the shears and garden saws in Mr. Fisher's tool shed.

Mr. Fisher gave him a troubled look. "And cut off your fingers as well, Master Bell."

"That isn't the plan," said Darius.

"And lose half the tools in the process. It's not that I don't trust you, Master Bell. Of course I do. But I'm not sure about this idea. Tools aren't toys."

"Daddy," said Marguerite, "I'll make sure they don't get lost."

The gardener looked at his daughter. "Are you in on this as well, Marguerite?"

Marguerite was. Darius had already spoken with her to make sure she would help him persuade her father. Mr. Fisher was as generous as the next person, or even more generous, but when it came to lending his tools, he was as cautious as the next person, as well. Yet he trusted Marguerite. He would even have trusted her to cut the asparagus shoots at the harvest if he wasn't able to do it himself.

"I'll make sure everything comes back," said Marguerite. "I promise."

Mr. Fisher frowned. Marguerite glanced at Darius and gave him a quick smile. Her father, she knew, found it hard to refuse anything to anybody, and hardest of all to refuse anything to her.

"What day are you doing it, Darius?" she said.

"Monday."

"Good," said Marguerite, ignoring the even more troubled look on her father's face. "We'll take the tools on Monday morning, and have them back by Monday night. That sounds all right, doesn't it, Daddy?"

After that, Darius just needed to organize enough kids. There were Oliver and Paul, of course, and together they thought of another half-dozen kids they could trust. They went to visit them and asked whether they were prepared to come and help, even though they couldn't be told what it was for – but when they saw what it was for, they'd be glad they'd agreed. Two refused. One had to go to visit his aunt in the country with his parents and couldn't make it. Three agreed to help. That would be enough, thought Darius, together with Paul and Oliver and Marguerite. And himself, of course.

After all of that, just when he thought everything was ready, Darius had one more idea. He didn't mention this to

Paul or to Oliver or to Marguerite. This, he decided, would be a surprise even to them.

He found Mrs. Simpson in the kitchen. He told her that he had a request, because he'd been thinking about what she had said the last time he came to the kitchen with Paul and Oliver – that a perfect cake could make a perfect occasion. And he had an occasion in mind which would be perfect for the perfect cake. But she didn't have to do it, he said, and he'd understand if she didn't, because it was a big request, and she might think it was presumptuous of him to ask. To which Mrs. Simpson said: "If you don't ask, you'll never know, will you?"

Exactly, thought Darius. And he was reminded of one of Paul Klasky's sayings. Nothing ventured, nothing gained.

So he told her what his idea was, and why, and as she listened, Mrs. Simpson's eyes went wider and wider with delight, and when he had finished, she said, "Of course, I'll do it. Darius Bell, I'm almost angry with you for even thinking I might say no!"

Chapter 20

The area of the estate around the jungle house was normally deserted, with nothing but the call of birds and the rustle of possums to disturb the silence. But on Monday it was abuzz with activity. Along the path from the gate in Roebuck Street children worked at the overgrowth, hacking off branches and snipping at shoots and tearing down vines with their bare hands. At lunchtime they stopped, and they ate out of a big picnic basket that Mrs. Simpson had prepared, full of sandwiches and fruit tarts, and then they kept going with renewed energy, clearing the track and throwing branches and vines into the undergrowth on either side.

It wasn't only along the track that there was activity. Mr.

Ostrovich had prepared the pieces of the barrier and handrail, and at ten o'clock he parked his truck outside the gate and unloaded them. Darius, Oliver and two of the other kids, Marcel Rouse and Hilary Engels, helped carry the pieces through the wood, while Marguerite, Paul and Donald Brill, the third kid who had agreed to help, continued to clear the path. Marcel, Hilary and Donald still didn't know what was inside the hole in the ground, and they watched in amazement as Mr. Ostrovich began taking the pieces down. His job was a lot easier than it might have been, because Mr. Bullwright had already spent a day working at the pool, and had cut a set of rough steps in the rock and had put in a light. Now he was building a three-foot-high brick wall around the entrance.

"What's down there?" asked Hilary.

"All will be revealed at the end of the day," said Darius mysteriously. Oliver grinned.

It wasn't until five o'clock that they had finished clearing the path. Mr. Ostrovich had finished his work and gone, and so had Mr. Bullwright.

"Now, do you want to see what it is?" asked Darius.

"No," replied Marcel Rouse sarcastically. "We're not interested at all."

"Come on, then," said Darius.

They headed for the hole in the ground.

"What *is* it?" asked Hilary impatiently.

"You know what they say," said Paul Klasky. "Good things come to those who wait."

"We've waited," muttered Donald Brill. "And we've worked as well!"

"And you won't be disappointed," said Darius. He led them into the hole and down the steps that Mr. Bullwright had cut in the rock. Everyone followed him.

They stopped in the darkness, with Mr. Ostrovich's railing keeping them from the water beyond. "Now," said Darius, "before I show you, I'm going to ask you to promise two things."

"Come *on*, Darius!" said Marcel. "How much longer are you going to keep us waiting?"

"Only until you promise."

"What is it, then?" demanded Hilary.

"First, not to say what you see down here to anyone who hasn't been here themselves."

"I'm starting to wonder whether there's really anything down here at all," muttered Marcel.

"And second, to invite all your friends to come and see it on Wednesday afternoon at two o'clock. Tell them to come to the gate in Roebuck Street and follow the signs."

"Wait a minute," said Hilary. "How can we tell them to come if we're not allowed to tell them what we see?"

"Tell them to come if you think it's worth seeing. You don't have to. Once I've shown you, if you don't think it's worth seeing, don't tell them to come. It's up to you. But if you do tell them to come, just don't say what you saw." Darius looked around. "All right?"

"All right already!" muttered Marcel. Hilary and Donald Brill nodded.

"That goes for everyone else, too," said Darius. "Paul? Oliver? Marguerite?"

They nodded as well.

"And if you do want to invite your friends to come," said Darius, "if you think it's worth it, tell them to invite their friends on Wednesday afternoon as well, and ask *their* friends to invite their friends."

"Darius…" growled Marcel.

Darius laughed. "All right. Then look!"

Darius pressed the switch to the light that Mr. Bullwright had installed.

There were gasps. Marcel and Hilary and Donald gazed, mouths open in amazement.

"But not a word about what you've seen," said Darius. "Remember your promise."

Darius and Marguerite took the tools back to Mr. Fisher.

"They're all there, Daddy," said Marguerite.

"And no one lost a finger," added Darius. "At least, I don't think anyone did."

"Did you count?" asked Mr. Fisher.

Darius laughed.

"Well, thank you for bringing them all back, Master Bell."

"No, thank you for lending them to us, Mr. Fisher."

Mr. Fisher turned to put the tools away in their places in the shed. "It'll be a busy day on Wednesday," he said as he hung up a pair of shears.

"Why's that, Mr. Fisher?" asked Darius.

"Your mother has asked us to do a special harvest. She wants a wheelbarrow full of vegetables, as a special favor, the very best we can find."

"Really?" said Darius.

"Apparently, they're for the Bell Gift, Master Bell. Of course, I don't expect they'll be the whole Gift. I'm not that foolish. There must be more, much more, that your father has prepared. But it's a nice touch, I think, to add some vegetables as well."

Darius glanced at Marguerite. They shared a smile. There was nothing more that Darius's father had prepared. But there was more that *they* had prepared.

"It's an honor, Master Bell, to be asked to provide part of the Gift," said the gardener, hanging up another pair of shears. "Even if it's as humble a part as some of my vegetables."

"There's nothing humble about your vegetables, Mr. Fisher. Even if we don't end up using them for the Gift, you shouldn't be disappointed. There's nothing humble about them at all."

Mr. Fisher turned around. "Do you think so, Master Bell?" Darius nodded.

The gardener smiled, and turned back to his tools.

Darius and Marguerite went outside.

There was just one more thing Darius needed to do before everything would be ready. "I have to put up signs tomorrow so people will know where they're meant to go. I've been thinking about it, but I don't know what to call it. *The Hole in the Ground*? Sounds silly."

"What about the Cave?" said Marguerite.

"I thought of that. I don't know, it still doesn't sound great."

"The Underground Pool?"

Darius shrugged.

"The Glittery Cave?"

"It's not catchy, is it?"

They thought, frowning in concentration.

"I know what to call it!" said Marguerite. "The Glitter Pool."

Chapter 21

The next morning, Darius's father announced that he wanted to speak with Darius and Cyrus in the yellow sitting room after they had finished breakfast. Perfect, thought Darius, because that was precisely what he had been going to suggest. The yellow sitting room was used for the most important family occasions. It was also used for the not-so-important family occasions, because of the almost-usable sofa it contained. Yet Darius couldn't imagine a more important occasion than announcing that a magnificent Bell Gift was ready to be given to the town.

Their father and mother were already waiting there when Darius and Cyrus came in. Hector Bell's face, which was normally so cheerful, was gloomy. Darius couldn't wait to see how it would change once he told him his news.

Darius and Cyrus sat on the sofa. For a moment they shifted and bounced around, until they found comfortable positions.

"Boys," said Darius's father solemnly, "I have something very grave to tell you. You need to prepare yourselves for tomorrow. It will be a very difficult day."

Darius struggled to keep the smile off his face. Difficult? It was going to be great!

"Tomorrow, as you know, is the day of the sixth Bell Gift. I have to admit something to you that I have, foolishly perhaps, been trying to conceal – we have no money for a real Gift. A statue, a spire, a bell, a fountain, a set of stained glass windows – all of these are beyond us."

Darius and Cyrus glanced at each other.

"And Cousin Julius, who I thought would be able to help, finds himself in unexpected difficulty and has been unable to assist. I admit, I thought he would ride to our rescue like a knight on his charger, like a warrior of old waving his shining banner, like a…" Darius's father's voice trailed off, as if he didn't have the will left for his high-flying rhetoric. "Anyway, he didn't. This must come as a shock to you, I realize."

Beside him, Darius's mother looked at her two sons, silently willing them not to reveal that they had realized all of this long ago.

"Papa," said Darius.

Darius's father waved his hand wearily. "Yes, I know, Darius. I've let you down. And you too, Cyrus. I'm very sorry about this. I'm ashamed. I have betrayed you both."

"No, Hector," said Darius's mother. "You don't feel like that, do you, boys?"

"Papa," said Darius, "you don't have to worry about any of this."

"Don't I?" said his father sadly.

"No. There's something I want to tell you."

Darius's father shook his head. "Darius, let me finish."

"But –"

"Darius, please."

"Darius," said his mother, "let your father speak."

Darius folded his arms. He'd let him speak, but wait until his father heard what Darius had to say after that!

Hector Bell drew a heavy sigh. "Well, despite all of this, a Gift must be given, or else the House will be taken away. And it must be given in person, by me, at midday tomorrow, in front of the entire city council." Darius's father paused. "Since there is nothing else we have to give – nothing of any value, in any event – I have asked Mr. Fisher to collect as many of his wonderful vegetables as he can, and I'll take these as the Gift, asking that they be distributed to the poor and needy in the town."

"This means, by the way, that we'll have fewer vegetables for the next few weeks," added Darius's mother, "because they'll have to come out of the share Mr. Fisher would have given us. But I think we can manage that, can't we?"

"Boys, can we?" asked Darius's father.

Darius and Cyrus nodded.

"Good boys. You're such good boys…" Their father's voice drifted off, and then he sighed again, and gave a small twitch, as if recollecting himself. "I don't expect you to come with me when I give the Gift, of course. I'm only telling you this because it will be a day of great humiliation for the Bell family, and naturally, even if you aren't there, I know it will affect you."

"People will talk," said Darius's mother.

"People *will* talk," said Darius's father. "Sadly, that is the way of the world. By tomorrow afternoon, I fear, the entire town will know, and after that our lives will never be the same."

Cyrus glanced at Darius. Their lives *wouldn't* be the same. In Cyrus's opinion, once the truth was out, once they didn't have to pretend that the Bell family was still wealthy and powerful, their lives would be better.

"You may be teased," said Darius's father.

Cyrus glanced at Darius again. As if they weren't teased already!

"The world is cruel, and never crueler than to those who have come down a notch. Delivering vegetables as the Gift is more than one notch, I think."

"But you don't have to do it, Papa!" said Darius.

Darius's father shook his head. "The House will be taken otherwise, Darius. We must face facts."

"But there's another way."

"Have you heard from Cousin Julius?" asked Darius's father quickly, and for a moment there was a glimmer of hope in his eyes.

Darius shook his head. "Papa, in the wood –"

"Darius, I know, you want me to sell it. It's noble of you to think of it, because I know how much you love it. You're a true Bell. And I would sell it if I could, but I can't. I should have told you. The Bell Grant doesn't allow us to sell any part of the estate."

"I know that! You don't have to sell it. There's something you can use to –"

"Nor can we use any part of it, Darius. No part of the land can be used in place of the Gift in any shape or form. The Grant is very specific – if we use part of the land for the Gift, we forfeit the estate, just as if we sold it. It's impossible."

"But you don't understand –"

"Darius, please. Don't go on. I know this is painful. It's as painful to me as it is to you." Hector Bell sighed deeply. "I must give the vegetables."

"No!"

Darius's father stood up. "I will do it alone. I don't want either of you exposed to the humiliation that I will bear."

"No, Papa," said Cyrus. "We'll come as well."

"Cyrus, Cyrus… That's very noble of you, but there's no need. I'm the one who's brought us to this point, therefore I should bear the responsibility." Darius's father was silent for a moment, frowning. "This isn't exactly the Gift I dreamed I would give, when I was your age, boys. I dreamed that when my time came I would give something truly extraordinary, truly magnificent, something that would live forever as a monument to the name of Bell…"

Darius's father stopped and shook his head, as if he couldn't quite believe, even now, what his dream had come to. Not every Bell had the chance to give a Gift, and for those who did, the opportunity came only once in a lifetime. For twenty-five years, since he had watched his own father give the fifth Gift, Hector Bell had waited for this day, imagining it would be the greatest day of his life. It would be his turn to uphold the honor of the family name, to take his place in the tradition of the Bells who had come before him. Now it was almost here. But instead of being the best day of his life, it was going to be the worst. He felt that he was betraying the name of every Bell who had ever lived, and he would never have a second chance to fix it. He sighed.

"Well, after this it'll be up to you. You'll do a better job than your father, eh? I only hope that when your turn comes, in another twenty-five years, you'll be able to restore the honor to our family name that tomorrow I will lose."

"There's no honor lost in this, Hector," said Darius's mother softly.

"That's right," said Cyrus. "If a wheelbarrow of vegetables is what we can give, then that's what we should give, and I, for one, am proud to give it. I don't mind being poor as long as we're honest."

Darius's father smiled sadly. He gazed at his sons with tears in his eyes. "Such good boys," he murmured. He glanced at his wife. "An honor to the name of Bell."

"We'll come with you," said Cyrus. "Won't we, Darius?"

"But we don't need to!"

"Exactly," said Darius's father. "I should do it alone."

He headed for the door.

"But you don't *need* to!" cried Darius again. "You don't need to! Why won't you listen?"

Darius jumped up, but Cyrus grabbed him and pinned him down. He put a hand over his mouth.

Darius struggled. He kept shouting, but Cyrus muffled his words.

Their father paused on his way out of the room. "That's right, boys. Enjoy yourselves. Have a wrestle! You don't know what good it does me to see you in such high spirits. It reminds me of myself and Cousin Julius in our younger days." He nodded, and sighed heavily once again, and went slowly out the door.

Darius's mother got up as well. "I know this is hard, Darius, but this is how it must be."

"But you don't understand!" cried Darius, kicking and struggling. Or that's what he thought he cried. Thanks to Cyrus's hand clamped down over his mouth and the effort he was making to struggle free, what came out was more like, "*Baauuonnnunnnerrraaaaaaaaaaaaandd!*"

Darius's mother shook her head sadly. "Try to accept it,

178

Darius," she said, and left the room.

Darius stopped struggling. He looked up at Cyrus. Slowly, Cyrus took his hand away.

"Why did you do that?" yelled Darius. "Let me go!"

Cyrus smirked.

"Let me go!"

Cautiously, Cyrus released him.

Darius turned and started beating him with his fists.

"Stop it!" yelled Cyrus, catching his hands. He held them tight. "Are you going to stop it?"

Darius squirmed.

"Are you?"

Darius was quiet.

Cyrus relaxed his grip on Darius's wrists.

Darius pulled himself loose and threw himself into the other corner of the sofa. "Why did you do that?" he demanded.

"Because you were just going to make things worse," said Cyrus. "Papa's decided to do it. That's the best thing that could happen. Whatever you had to say, all it could do was make things harder for him."

"How do you know?"

"Because there isn't anything else, is there? What else can he do? There isn't any alternative to Mr. Fisher's vegetables."

"Yes, there is! That's what I was trying to say. It's ready, Cyrus. It's all ready!"

"What is?"

"The Glitter Pool."

"The what?"

"The place I took you! The hole in the ground! The Glitter Pool!"

Darius told him what he had done, the way he had gotten everyone to help, the way it had been prepared.

"You did all that?" said Cyrus.

"Yes! That's what I was trying to tell them! I had it all planned, but you had to interfere. Well, it doesn't matter.I'm going to tell them now."

Darius got up.

"Wait," said Cyrus.

"What is it now?"

"Darius, you heard what Papa said. The Grant says you can't use the land in place of the Gift."

"It's not *using* the land. It's a hole, Cyrus. We didn't make it, it opened up by itself. How can that be using the land? And we're not making any money from it. It's just showing what's there!"

"But people might say it's using it."

"But I would say it isn't!"

Cyrus frowned thoughtfully. "It's a question of definition."

"Who's to say my definition's wrong?" demanded Darius.

"That's a good question," murmured Cyrus. He was silent for a moment, still thinking. "Did you really organize all of that?" he asked eventually.

"How many times do I have to tell you? Do you want to see it? There are steps, there are lights. I'll show you if you like!"

Cyrus frowned again. "You know that I think it's best for Papa to go with a wheelbarrow of vegetables, if that's all we can give."

"I know that," said Darius bitterly.

"But…"

Darius waited.

"The fact that he's got to this point, that he's had to face it … maybe that's enough."

"He's not in denial," said Darius, "if that's what you mean."

"No, he's not. And the Glitter Pool, as you call it – that *would* be a Gift. That would be something. People would come to see it."

"Who comes to see the statue of Great-great-great-great-great-grandfather Cornelius?"

"No one."

"No one but the pigeons. And the Gift doesn't have to be in Founders Square."

"True. That's just a tradition."

"Traditions are made to be broken."

Cyrus nodded thoughtfully. "But we have to be careful, Darius. If we gave a Gift and it was regarded as using the land, we'd forfeit the House. Podcock would take it, he's just waiting for something like this. It's not a game. We can't take a chance."

"I thought you didn't care if we lost the House."

"Of course I care, Darius! I care as much as you do. Don't

be such a waste of… I care, all right?" Cyrus frowned. "It would depend on the words, as to whether we'd be using the land or not. The exact words of the Grant. We have to find out before we say anything to Papa. It would kill him if we got his hopes up and then it turned out he'd have to give the vegetables anyway. We have to know *exactly* what the Grant says."

That was true, thought Darius. He watched his brother. Cyrus was thinking about something, he could see that. Darius waited. This was his last chance, he knew. His last hope.

"Have you ever seen the Grant?" he asked.

Cyrus shook his head. He had heard about it all his life, just as he had heard about Cousin Julius, but he had never laid eyes on it.

Yet there was one important difference between Cousin Julius and the Bell Grant.

Cyrus smiled. "I know where it is."

Chapter 22

Bungle, Whistler and Drape had been the lawyers for the Bell family since the days of Cornelius Bell, and in the same measure that the Bell family had grown poorer, so the lawyers had grown wealthier. Just as it was a Bungle who had placed a copy of the Bell Grant in the lawyers' safe on the day that it had been issued to Cornelius Bell, so now it was the great-great-great-grandson of that same Bungle who took it out of the safe and placed it on the desk in front of Cyrus and Darius.

The lawyer sat down behind his desk, glanced at the clock, and noted the time on a yellow notepad. He was a round man with a cheerful demeanor and a pair of rimless spectacles on his nose. "Now, young gentlemen," he said. "Here is the Grant, what is the matter?" He chuckled. "That's a legal term. Matter, I mean. It doesn't mean anything's actually the matter."

Darius glanced at Cyrus and rolled his eyes.

"It's about the Bell Gift," said Cyrus.

"Due tomorrow, if I'm not mistaken," said Bungle, and he picked up the Grant and turned its pages. "Yes. At twelve o'clock."

"We know that," said Darius.

"Problem solved!" announced Bungle cheerfully.

"Not exactly, Mr. Bungle," said Cyrus.

"No?" Bungle's face was troubled. "Twelve o'clock, young sir. This is what it says. All the town is waiting to find out what it is. A gift of quite exceptional magnificence is expected. Mayor Podcock has been telling everyone that it will be quite the most spectacular Gift yet." Bungle leaned forward confidentially. "No one quite knows how it's possible, given that Hector Bell doesn't have two cents to rub together… I mean your father, as it were…" Bungle stopped and blinked a couple of times. "Yes, well, there we are."

"It *will* be the most magnificent Gift," said Cyrus.

Darius looked at him in surprise. Cyrus nodded, then turned back to Bungle.

"There's only one slight problem. It's on the estate."

"On the estate, you say?"

Cyrus nodded.

"Well, who cares?" said the lawyer.

"Mr. Bungle, I think you should check the Grant."

"Should I?"

Cyrus nodded.

Bungle picked up the Grant again and began to scan it. He turned over one page, then another.

Cyrus and Darius waited.

"Ahhh…" said Bungle. "I see what you mean. Here boys, look."

Bungle pushed the Grant across the desk. Then he put his stubby finger down on the paper, about halfway down the page.

"Clause 3, subclause ii, section d."

Darius read, craning his neck to see the words around Bungle's finger.

d) A presentation of the usage of the land of the Estate will be deemed to be not a Gift under the terms of the Grant, whether the usage be in whole or in part, for a fixed term or an open term or a term in perpetuity, for trade or entertainment or for any other use or in any other arrangement or for any other purpose not herein mentioned or in future to be developed;

"Well," said Bungle, "I think that's clear."

"Is it?" said Darius.

Bungle picked up the document and read it again. "I think it is. Admirably."

"But we don't want to use the land," said Darius. "We just want to show people what's there."

"Sounds like trade," said the lawyer.

"But we won't be charging them," said Cyrus.

"Sounds like entertainment."

"But it won't do any harm!" said Darius.

"Sounds irrelevant," said the lawyer. "*Or for any other use or in any other arrangement or for any other purpose not herein mentioned or in future to be developed.* Sounds comprehensive, don't you think? In fact, I can't imagine how you could do anything with the land that wouldn't fall under that prohibition. I'm sorry, young gentlemen. Very little to be done, I'm afraid."

"But all we want to do is take people down some steps under the ground and show them something," said Darius.

"The Grant doesn't care what you want –" Bungle stopped. "What did you say?"

"We just want to show them something."

"No. Before that. Something about under the ground."

"We just want to take them down some steps under the ground."

"That was it! How many steps?"

"A few."

"How far under the ground?"

Darius looked at Cyrus.

"Ten or twelve feet," said his brother.

"Ten or twelve feet," said Bungle. He repeated it to himself, and again, leafing quickly through the Grant. He stopped on one of the pages towards the end. "Hmmm…" He looked up. "You may have a case. This Grant is for the land. It becomes a question," said Bungle, raising a finger, "of whether that includes what is under the land."

"How do we answer that question?" said Darius.

"That, young sir, is another question." Bungle stood up. "Two heads are better than one, I think. And as we say at Bungle, Whistler and Drape, four heads are better than two. Excuse me for a moment."

Bungle went out. A moment later he came back with a man who looked just like him, only greyer, and thinner, and older.

"Mr. Bungle, my father," he announced, "one of the greatest lawyers of his day, and still a deft hand in court."

The elder Bungle shook his head, beaming with pleasure. "You're too kind, Bernard."

"Nonsense, Father. This is Master Bell and Master Bell."

"Ah, Bells!" said the elder Bungle. He held out his hand to Cyrus and then to Darius. "I hope we'll be seeing very much more of you in the future."

"Sit, Father," said the younger Bungle, pulling out a chair for the older man. Then he sat down behind the desk, glanced at the clock, and noted the time on his yellow pad. "I'll explain the matter," he said.

A minute after he had done that, the door opened again. In walked a tall man with curly black hair and a tic affecting one eye.

"Mr. Drape," said the younger Bungle, "a great expert who can help in the case."

"Too kind, Bungle, too kind," said Drape.

Bungle looked at the clock, noted the time, and explained the matter again.

Then the door opened and in walked a Whistler. And then another Drape. And then a Bungle who was a cousin of the two Bungles already in the room. As each of them came in, the original Bungle looked at the clock, noted the time and explained the matter again. Finally there were eight lawyers, six clerks and a cleaning lady who had come in to see what the fuss was about, all vigorously debating the issue.

Suddenly, there was silence.

"We're agreed," said the original Bungle.

"I wouldn't go that far," said a Drape.

"You have a case. By practice, usage of the land refers to the surface of the land, extending not more than three feet beneath the surface."

"Five feet," objected Drape, his tic-affected eye blinking furiously. "Go back to your books, Bungle. Look up *Hollingworth v. Gruberschnatz*." He glanced at Darius and Cyrus. "A most fascinating case."

"Provided the thing you want to show is deeper than this," said Bungle, "you could use it for the Gift."

"Excellent!" said Darius.

"It's certainly more than five feet below the surface," said Cyrus.

"Then I concur," said the Drape who had objected. "You may use it as you wish."

"Even as the Gift?" said Cyrus.

"Indeed."

Darius grinned. Finally! They were going to be able to do it!

"You just won't be able to get there over the land," said one of the Whistlers, a broad-shouldered woman with heavy dark eyebrows.

"We won't *what*?" said Cyrus.

"Well, I'm presuming this thing, whatever it is, is within the estate," replied the Whistler. "While you can use the thing that is under the ground, if anyone crosses the land to get there, that is a usage of the land, and therefore prohibited."

"You mean no one can walk across the land to get there?" asked Darius.

"Or crawl," said Whistler. "Or skip, or roll, or do anything else of a locomotive nature connected to the seeing of this thing that you are showing."

"But how are they meant to get there?"

"That is not the law's concern."

"Then the law's ridiculous!"

"Precisely," said the elder Bungle, and he smiled nostalgically.

"All is not lost, Master Bell," said the younger Bungle, holding up a finger dramatically. "We have thought about this. There are a couple of solutions. If you had a bridge over the land from which someone could go down into the hole, for example, that would be a way to do it."

"Provided, of course, that the legs of the bridge did not stand on the land itself, because that would be a usage," said Whistler.

"You mean the bridge would have to go from one side of the estate to the other without touching any of it?" said Cyrus.

"Precisely."

Darius glanced at his brother. Cyrus shook his head. There were bridges with single spans of that length that had been built – and with what it cost to build them, you could have bought a thousand Bell Gifts.

"And the person coming down from the bridge couldn't touch the land," added Bungle cheerfully. "But he would be allowed to do it, for example, if he came down straight into the hole."

"And how would he do that?" asked Darius.

"We're lawyers, Mr. Bell, not engineers. But I hazard a guess that if you hung a rope from the bridge directly into the hole and the person went down it – not touching the edges of the hole itself, of course, which would be a usage – then it could be done."

"And how would he get back up?"

"By the rope!" declared Bungle.

"A small motor could be used to raise the person," said one of the clerks. "I believe such motors are readily available at reasonable cost. In fact, I know of…"

The clerk stopped. All the lawyers were glaring at him.

Bungle coughed. "A small motor, Master Bell."

"And the other option?" asked Darius quietly.

"A tunnel!" announced Drape. "More than five feet deep."

"And I suppose that would have to go all the way from the outside of the estate?" said Darius.

"Naturally."

Darius glanced at Cyrus. Cyrus shrugged. Tunnels weren't cheap, either.

The lawyers beamed at them.

"Thank you," said Darius. "You've been the most helpful bunch of lawyers ever."

"Too kind, too kind," muttered the elder Bungle, while his son looked at the clock and noted the time.

Outside, Darius and Cyrus stopped on the sidewalk. Cyrus shook his head in disbelief. But Darius couldn't bring himself even to smile at the lawyers' antics. This was it, he knew. It was over. There was nothing more to be done. Mr. Podcock wouldn't let them get away with anything. If the Gift involved usage of the land, in any shape, in any form, they would lose the House. And unless they could suddenly build a bridge with one of the longest spans in the world, or excavate a tunnel under the estate by the next morning, there was no way the Glitter Pool could be the Gift.

"You know, everything you've done, Darius, it doesn't have to go to waste. It's amazing, really."

Darius didn't reply. It was the second time in a week that Cyrus had openly admired something that Darius had done.

And for the second time in a week, it came at a time when Darius was so disappointed, so discouraged, that he didn't care.

Darius thought of the ordeal his father was going to have to endure the next day.

"People can still see it, Darius. It just can't be the Gift, that's all."

Darius shrugged. "Then what's the point?"

Chapter 23

The truck drew up outside the town hall in Founders Square a few minutes before twelve o'clock. Out of one side got Mr. Fisher and out of the other Darius's father, dressed in his best suit, which was at least ten years old. They went to the back of the truck. Mr. Fisher opened the doors, set up a plank from the truck down to the street, went into the back and rolled out a wheelbarrow full of vegetables.

There were zucchini, lettuces, tomatoes, red peppers, green peppers, radishes, spring onions, red cabbages, white cabbages, cucumbers, cauliflowers, carrots, eggplant, broccoli and two bunches of asparagus, all in the ripest condition. They gleamed with freshness.

Darius's father sighed, gazing at them.

"They're fine vegetables, Mr. Bell," said the gardener.

"Indeed they are, Mr. Fisher. If you find me somewhat downcast, it's not on account of the produce."

"Those who have them will be lucky, Mr. Bell."

"Indeed they will be, Mr. Fisher," replied Darius's father, and he sighed again.

The Bells' old yellow car pulled up behind the truck. Out got Darius's mother, Cyrus and Darius.

Darius's father turned to them. "Micheline," he said seriously, "for the last time, the boys needn't come. Nor you, my dear."

"I don't think we'd care to miss it, Hector," replied Darius's mother. "Such fine vegetables. To see them given away would be a privilege."

Darius's father opened his mouth to speak, but the words didn't come out. He looked at his two sons, his eyes moist with emotion. Darius smiled, and his father forced a smile to his lips in return.

"Very well," he said. He drew himself up to his full height, threw back his shoulders and said, "Bells, let us give the Gift!"

For a moment, he maintained his bearing, but when he looked down again and saw the reality – a wheelbarrow, a load of vegetables, in place of the magnificent Gift he had always dreamed of giving – his shoulders slumped. "I'll take it now, Mr. Fisher," he said quietly.

The gardener nodded and stepped away from the

wheelbarrow.

"They really are lovely vegetables, Mr. Fisher," said Darius's mother. "You've made an excellent selection."

"Thank you, Mrs. Bell."

Darius's father drew a deep breath. Then he gripped the handles of the wheelbarrow, raised them, and began pushing.

Mr. Fisher picked up the plank and hurried to lay it on the steps of the town hall before Hector Bell reached them. Then the gardener watched as Darius's father pushed the wheelbarrow up the steps and into the building. Micheline, Cyrus and Darius followed.

Through the lobby of the town hall he went. Each pace was like the blow of a whip for Hector Bell, each step a step closer to his utter humiliation. His shoulders sagged lower and lower. And yet he kept going, followed by his wife and two sons, pushing the wheelbarrow of his shame across the marble floor. People watched as he went past, their faces first showing surprise, then amusement.

At the door of the council chamber, Darius's father stopped.

The usher looked down at the wheelbarrow and smirked.

"Please announce that Hector Bell has arrived with the Bell Gift," said Darius's father. His voice was so low that the usher could barely hear it.

"Where is it?" said the usher.

Darius's father almost managed not to flinch. It was only the first cruel joke, he knew, that would be made at his expense. The laughter hadn't even begun.

"Please announce it," he said hoarsely.

The usher's lip curled in disdain. He opened the door behind him, and announced in a loud voice to the chamber beyond: "Hector Bell craves admission with the Bell Gift."

Darius saw his father wince at the words. He had never seemed more like a child to Darius than at that moment, vulnerable, easily injured, as he waited before the door of the council chamber to be invited in with his wheelbarrow of vegetables.

Yet he had to wait a minute longer, enduring the derisive grin of the usher. Finally the chimes of the Bell Bell struck midday.

"Invite Hector Bell to come forward," came a voice from within the chamber.

The usher stepped aside and waved his arm towards the open door, bowing almost to the ground in an extravagant, mocking gesture.

Darius's father remained rooted to the spot. The chamber stretched out in front of him now, unobstructed, and directly opposite, at the other end of the hall, sat George Podcock on the mayoral throne.

"Hector," murmured Darius's mother, and she nudged him gently.

Darius's father gave a start. "Yes. Of course. Sorry."

Darius's mother nudged him again. Hector Bell took a deep breath, closed his eyes for an instant, then raised the handles of the wheelbarrow and pushed it forward.

He advanced into the chamber. On either side of him sat the councilors. Behind them, in rows of seats rising to the wall, were the public galleries. People had come to see the giving of the Gift, excited by rumors of a stupendous donation that the Mayor had been spreading. One part of the galleries was reserved for the press, and it was packed with journalists.

There was a puzzled silence as Darius's father advanced with the wheelbarrow before him. After Micheline, Cyrus and Darius had followed him in, the usher closed the door behind them. A moment later he opened it a fraction and peered through the crack.

Darius's father stopped about halfway along the chamber. He let down the handles of the wheelbarrow. Through the stained glass windows that had been given by his father, the light played pink and yellow and blue across the vegetables.

Cameras clicked as the photographers amongst the journalists took pictures. By now people in the chamber were starting to think this was some kind of joke that Hector Bell was playing. From the galleries came a ripple of laughter. Darius's father stood silent, staring at the floor somewhere between him and the mayoral throne.

Another usher stood beside the mayor. "Order!" he boomed. "Order in the chamber!"

The laughter died away. George Podcock stood up.

"Mr. Bell," he said, "I welcome you to the council chamber.

What is your business?"

"I am here to present the sixth Bell Gift," replied Darius's father.

The mayor gazed at him. The corner of his mouth lifted in a sneer. "Proceed," he said, and sat down.

Darius's father tried to avoid Podcock's eyes, yet couldn't help but glimpse them as the mayor sat waiting, almost greedily, for what was to come.

"Mr. Mayor," said Darius's father, "honorable councilors, ladies and gentlemen of the public. It is the long-accepted requirement and tradition that in each generation the Bell family shall provide a gift to the city in recognition of the city's generosity in granting the estate of Bell House to Cornelius Bell, who was my great-great-great-great-grandfather. Today, that joyful day has come again, and it is my privilege to be the Bell who answers the call. Accordingly, I stand before the council to discharge this welcome obligation." Somehow he had managed to speak strongly until this moment, but now his voice faltered. Hector Bell clenched his teeth, then forced himself to go on. "As the sixth Bell Gift, I present to the city this wheelbarrow of fine vegetables, and I humbly ask that the council sees to it that they are distributed to those who are genuinely needy and hungry in our midst."

There was a moment of stunned silence, then some wag in the public gallery called out, "Looks like you should keep them yourself, then." Suddenly everyone realized that the vegetables, in fact, were the Gift. There was a roar of laughter.

The people on the public benches pointed and laughed, journalists chuckled and shook their heads as they made notes, and the councilors themselves, unable and unwilling to hold back their mirth, grinned and giggled, whispering to each other and giggling some more. Only the usher beside the mayor, who took any kind of disorder as a personal affront, scowled at the noise and stepped forward to demand quiet. But the mayor restrained him. A little laughter, thought Podcock, was just what was wanted.

Hector Bell stood on the floor of the chamber as the giggles and the laughter and the wheezes rose around him. The mayor grinned from ear to ear. Suddenly Darius knew that he had never felt real hatred before, not such as he felt now for George Podcock.

Finally Podcock rose with a swagger and held up his hands for silence. He nodded his head curtly in the direction of Darius's father.

"May I thank you," he said, "on behalf of the city, for this *generous* gift." He paused as a ripple of derision swept around the chamber. "May I ask you, Mr. Bell, is it only the vegetables you are giving, or does your gift include the wheelbarrow as well?"

There were shrieks of enjoyment at this, and the council chamber echoed with laughter.

"If so, Mr. Bell," continued the mayor, savoring every second of the encounter, "since you have been so kind as to suggest to whom we should give the vegetables, to whom would you suggest we give the wheelbarrow?" Podcock paused for effect. "A needy bricklayer, perhaps? A destitute builder?"

The chamber thundered with laughter.

"Mr. Bell?"

"The wheelbarrow isn't included," said Darius's father quietly.

"What's that, Mr. Bell?" Podcock put his hand behind his ear for effect. "Can't you hear you, I'm afraid."

"The wheelbarrow…"

"Yes?"

"It isn't included."

"Shame," replied Podcock. "Myself, I was thinking we could have put it in the Square. Put it on a plinth opposite the statue of your ancestor. Would have looked lovely, don't you think?"

"Splendid!" cried one of the councilors in the uproar.

"*Alas*," roared Podcock above the noise, "*it's only the vegetables!*"

He came forward. The chamber quieted. It seemed to Darius that every face was grinning, leering, as if at some kind of performance, as if the next round was about to begin and the spectators were eager to see what taunt the mayor was going to make now.

Darius's father stood like a man who had been hit once, hit twice, yet knew he had to stand and wait to be hit again.

The mayor stood over the wheelbarrow. "So it's just the vegetables, then, is it?" he said.

"Yes," murmured Darius's father. "Just the vegetables."

"Well, Mr. Bell, in this chamber whose magnificent windows, one might note, were provided by none other than your own father, I thank you on behalf of the entire city for this … *radish*…" he picked up a radish by its stalk and waved it around the chamber, to roars of amusement, then dropped it in the wheelbarrow. "And this *cabbage*… And this lovely piece of *broccoli*… And this bunch of *tomatoes*… And this most excellent *lettuce*…"

The mayor went through the vegetables in the wheelbarrow, raising them for all to see. Darius's father stood with his head bowed, wincing as Podcock announced the name of each one. Then one of the carrots that the mayor had picked up fell on the floor. At that, something in Hector Bell seemed to change. Slowly his head came up, and Darius saw his father gazing directly now at the mayor who was still raising the vegetables and naming them and tossing them aside. Finally Podcock stopped, as if it was just too easy to make fun of Hector Bell and it was all getting rather boring.

Silently, Darius's father bent down and picked up the carrot that the mayor had dropped and placed it gently back on the wheelbarrow.

Then he straightened up again.

"It is a very ungracious man who mocks a gift," he said quietly.

The mayor stared at him.

"There may be little that I can give, Mr. Podcock, but

however little I have, at least I always have my manners."

There was a hush in the chamber now. Out of the corner of his eye, Darius noticed one of the journalists sitting forward in her seat, head cocked to hear the exchange. She had been laughing earlier, like everybody else, but now, as Darius's father spoke, she nodded, and wrote something down on her notepad.

The mayor bristled. "Perhaps you should have kept your vegetables and given us a gift of your manners then, Mr. Bell," he hissed.

"Well, Mr. Podcock, this gift is for the city, and yet I doubt after today that there is anyone in our city who requires a gift of manners quite as much as you do, sir."

There was a gasp in the chamber.

Everything about Darius's father was changing. He drew himself up straight, he threw back his shoulders, he looked the mayor in the eye.

Darius glanced at his brother. He saw Cyrus watching his father in a way that he had never seen before, with a look of approval. More than approval: respect.

"This is a small gift, Mr. Podcock. I wish I could give more, but it is all I could give. I admit it." Hector Bell looked around the chamber, first one side, then the other, then turned back to the mayor. "The person who mocks another for the smallness of his gift, it seems to me, is smaller than any gift could possibly ever be. This is a gift of food. True, it will not be here in fifty years, or a hundred years, like the other

Gifts, and I wish that it could be. I wish it could be a gift of food that would last forever, so there would never more be hunger in our city. Alas, I am not rich enough for such a Gift, nor to give more than this wheelbarrow full of vegetables that I have offered. Yet it is something, at least. Today there will be some families in our city who will be less hungry than they might have been but for this gift, and who but an exceedingly small person, would consider this a small thing? And in case you wonder, yes, everything you see in this wheelbarrow is taken out of my family's mouth. I thought this would be something to be ashamed of, but now I rather wonderfully find that I have no shame at all in admitting it. There is no wealth in my house, Mr. Podcock. There! Now mock me, sir, because it seems that wealth is the only measure you have for a person. For my part, I thank you, Mr. Podcock, for your mockery. You have performed a great service for me today."

"What is that?" whispered Podcock, almost too embarrassed to speak.

"I came here in shame. I came here thinking this is a very small Gift. But you, Mr. Podcock, have made it seem very large indeed."

Darius's father gazed at the mayor for one moment more, then turned and walked away.

Darius watched his father go past him. If he had never seemed more like a vulnerable child when he went into the chamber, he had never seemed a stronger, more dignified and more admirable man than when he walked out. Cyrus and

Micheline went after him. Darius stood for a moment longer before he followed them. He wanted to get one last look at the faces of the people in the chamber. He wanted them to see that he was looking at them. They avoided his eyes, as if they too had been shamed, like the mayor, for their laughter.

Darius turned and went. He walked out just as he had seen his father walk, head back, chest out, the walk of a Bell who may have lost his pretense of wealth, but had gained more, much more in dignity.

Nothing else was needed. After what his father had said, nothing else seemed necessary.

Not even the Glitter Pool.

Chapter 24

It wasn't necessary, and as they arrived home, Darius realized that that was the point.

The Glitter Pool didn't need to be the Gift. Suddenly he was glad that it wasn't, because any gift is better when given out of choice rather than requirement. And that was how the Glitter Pool was being given, not because it had to be, but because it could be.

But first, he had some explaining to do!

"What's going on?" asked Darius's father, stopping the car before he turned into the main gate and peering down Roebuck Street. "There are children everywhere!"

There were. Not ten, or twenty – as Darius had thought

might come, if they were lucky – nor fifty, nor even a hundred, but more. Many more. Those who had seen the Glitter Pool had spread the word, and despite the fact that they didn't say what they had seen – or because of it, perhaps, because there's nothing that piques the interest so much as a mystery – those they had told had spread the word in their turn. Take six people, and each one tells his or her friends. And they tell their friends. And they tell their friends. Before you know it, you'll have half the city on your doorstep.

Which is just what it looked like. And they hadn't waited until two o'clock to arrive. Once the excitement had spread, everyone wanted to be the first to see whatever it was that was supposed to be so special. Some of them had been waiting for hours outside the closed gate in Roebuck Street.

"Has someone set up a circus down there?" asked Darius's father.

"Not exactly," said Cyrus. "I think Darius can explain."

Both his parents looked at him.

"No one else was meant to be here yet," said Darius. "I wanted to show you first."

"Then I think you'd better hurry," said his mother.

They got out of the car at the House. Darius led them to the wood, without divulging what they were going to see. Like everyone else, his parents grew more and more intrigued. But he really did want it to be a surprise. He wanted to see the faces of his parents light up at the sight of the cavern's roof.

But they stopped in astonishment even before that, when

they saw the wall that Mr. Bullwright had built and the sign Darius had put up outside the entrance to the cavern.

"The Bell Glitter Pool?" said Darius's mother. "What's that?"

"I'll show you."

Darius took them down, warning them where they had to stoop to get into the cavern. Then he switched on the light.

Cyrus glanced at Darius and smiled. Their parents' faces were full of wonder.

"I was going to suggest that we open this up to everybody," said Darius. "In fact, I thought we might have given it as the Gift."

"But Mr. Bungle said we'd need to build a bridge over the land to get to it," added Cyrus, "or else it would be usage of the estate."

"Bungle?" said Darius's father dismissively. "Which Bungle? The younger or the elder?"

"Both."

"Well, neither of them knows anything, so it doesn't matter." Hector Bell laughed, and gazed around the cavern with amazement, taking in the glittering array of crystals.

"It's vanadinite and limonite," said Darius. "And wulfenite. And the gold isn't gold, it's fool's gold."

"Indeed?" said his father.

"I had it checked. By a professor."

"Indeed? Well, it doesn't matter to a literary man. Eh, Cyrus? That's more for a scientific fellow like yourself. To me, call it what you like, it's all rubies and gold."

He looked at Cyrus. Cyrus grinned.

"And as for you, Darius…"

Darius waited.

"The true Bell is the Bell who never gives up. Imagination! Daring! Courage! Think of the great Bells. Cornelius Bell. Lucius Bell. Achilles Bell."

"Darius Bell," said his mother.

"Indeed," said his father, "Darius Bell." He gazed at his son, eyes moist, reflecting the dazzling glitter of the cavern.

Darius could tell there was going to be a short story out of this. In fact, he half imagined that his father was already composing the opening lines in his head.

Suddenly his father frowned. "But we have guests! They're waiting!"

They were. Crowded around the side gate and halfway back along Roebuck Street.

Darius went quickly up the cleared path.

"That way," he said when he had opened the gate, pointing down the path. But the first of the kids were already past him and he had to run to catch up.

His parents were standing at the entrance to the Glitter Pool when they arrived. "Welcome," boomed his father, and then he kept up a constant line of chatter as the children went past him and down the stairs. "This way! Not too fast. Hello. Welcome. How nice you could come. Let's be patient. So pleased to see you. Why don't we wait a moment for the others to come out? Everyone will have a chance to see. Let's form a line."

Darius and Cyrus watched him.

"Look at him," said Cyrus, shaking his head. "Just like he owns the place."

"He does own the place," said Darius. "He's back to normal, that's all."

"Is he? I think it's more than that."

Darius glanced at his brother. He could see real respect in Cyrus's eyes, the respect he thought he had glimpsed in the council chamber.

"Papa was a brave man today, Darius. When I said it would be good for him, I don't know if I really thought about what it would take. I don't know if I could have been so brave in his position."

Darius looked at his brother in surprise. "I'm sure you could be, Cyrus."

Cyrus shrugged, as if he wasn't certain of it. "And there's something I need to say to you as well. You know I've often said you're a waste of –"

Suddenly Darius's eyes went wide. "I almost forgot!"

"What?"

"You'll see," said Darius, and he ran off before Cyrus could finish saying what he had started.

He went all the way back to the House. Marguerite was waiting. "Sorry!" he said, and they went down to the kitchen. On the table stood a cake that Mrs. Simpson had baked. She had insisted on making it a cake of enormous size, saying that when you didn't know how many guests you were going to have, always assume the most, and no one will be disappointed. Darius was glad that she had! The cake was in the shape of a bell, made out of sponge cake, layered with cream, covered in chocolate and festooned with gold icing and lumps of red candy. A Glitter Cake.

"People will remember this one, Mrs. Simpson!"

"I just hope they enjoy it, Darius," said the cook, but Darius didn't know how they possibly couldn't.

He and Marguerite carried it carefully on a folding table, while Mrs. Simpson came after them with bags full of napkins and paper plates.

When they got to the Glitter Pool, some of the children had already been down, and others were still waiting for their turn. A cheer went up when they saw the cake.

Darius's father was supposed to cut it. But now that he was back to his normal self, of course, he couldn't cut it without making a speech, using three words when one would do. He spent five minutes thanking Darius and everyone else who had helped to prepare the Glitter Pool, and ten minutes describing the pool itself, which had so discombobulated him with its beauty, he said, and so disconcerted him with its effect, and so disorientated him with its intricacy, that in short, in sum, in conclusion, he found himself almost speechless – but not quite, of course, as everyone could hear. And then he got so carried away by the occasion that he said the Glitter Pool would be open every year on this day, and anyone could come and see it. With cake provided. And then, just as he finally raised the knife to cut the cake, with everyone impatiently waiting for the talking to end and the eating to begin, he stopped again, and called Darius forward, and held out the knife to him, yet didn't quite hand it over, as he spent another five minutes describing why Darius ought to be the one to do the honors. Then at last he handed over the knife – encouraged by the fact that Darius decided to take it – and Darius cut the cake. Mrs. Simpson grabbed the knife and began slicing pieces before his father could say anything else. Everyone surged forward to get a piece, and Darius and his father found themselves caught in the middle of the throng, so Mrs. Simpson put a piece of cake each in their hands and they ate it right there, grinning at each other, as children gobbled cake all around them.

Darius forced his way out of the crowd. He stopped in surprise. There, standing right in front of him, was Professor Heggarty.

"Professor," he said. "What are you doing here?"

"I came to see the Glitter Pool."

"But you've seen it already."

"Does that mean I can't see it again?"

"Of course not. I'm just … surprised."

"I've already said hello to Mr. Klasky and Mr. Roberts, by the way."

Darius looked around. Paul and Oliver waved back, grinning, their hands covered with chocolate icing.

"I heard what your father said just now. It sounds as if you've done quite a thing here, Darius. But I suppose I shouldn't be surprised at a boy who isn't afraid to come looking for a professor when he's made a discovery."

"Are you angry at me?"

"Not at all. I was wondering if you were angry at *me* for showing you that you didn't have rubies and gold."

"It was just the truth, Professor. You can't be angry at the truth. Have you come to take more samples?"

Professor Heggarty shook her head. "My nephew mentioned that he was going to see something at Bell House. Something under the ground. That's him over there." She pointed towards a small, chocolate-smeared boy who was standing in the line to go down to the pool. "He'd heard it was the most amazing and beautiful thing, although he didn't know what it was. But I had a fair idea."

"More than a fair idea, Professor."

"Well, I thought I'd just come back and remind myself how beautiful it really is. Sometimes, when you're doing my kind of work, you can forget to just appreciate the beauty of what's in front of you."

Darius smiled.

"And actually, after I've seen it, I think I might have some cake as well."

Darius laughed. "If there's any left!"

"That's true. Perhaps I should get some on the way down."

Professor Heggarty went off to get a piece of cake and join

her nephew in the line.

Darius found his mother and his brother standing nearby.

"Who was that?" asked his mother.

"No one," said Darius. "She just came to look at the Glitter Pool and see how beautiful it is."

"Well, I almost can't believe you did all this yourself."

"I had help."

"Not from me," said Cyrus. "I can't claim any of the credit, not even for thinking of it. It was all your idea, wasn't it, Darius?"

"Well, Darius, it's quite an exceptional thing," said his mother.

Cyrus nodded. "You're not a complete waste of space, after all."

"Cyrus!" said his mother. "What a thing to say! Your brother's not a waste of space at all."

"Isn't that what I just said?"

Darius couldn't keep the smile off his face.

"Just don't let it go to your head," said Cyrus.

"No," said Darius, and he tried to look very serious. For about two seconds.

They watched the children, still going up and down the stairs, still going back for more cake, with Darius's father in the middle of the throng, directing.

"You know, I'm glad Bungle told you we couldn't give this as the Gift," said Darius's mother. "Some things are too beautiful to be given out of obligation. They should only be given out of love." She looked at Darius. "Or do you think that's silly?"

"No," said Darius. "I think that's right."

"Besides," said his mother, and she smiled mischievously, "I think a wheelbarrow full of vegetables was just what George Podcock and his council deserved."